PRAISE FOR *GROUND SWEET AS SUGAR*

Epic historical fiction at its best! Richly woven tale, which transported me back in time, travelling from Ireland to the West Indies. With powerful characters, I felt totally immersed in their lives. Feeling the toil and emotions of Charlotte as the story untangled her mysterious past, I turned page after page unable to put the story aside. — ***Review***

History meets one brilliant imagination in this epic tale! — ***For the Love of a Book***

A sweeping, epic, page turning adventure that I could not put down. Every imaginable element fills its delectable pages: suspense, romance, friendship, loyalty, adventure… The descriptions are mesmerizing. The characters layered. The writing style one of a kind. I loved it! — ***Author A.R. Hadley***

This entire story from start to finish held me captive… I was completely caught up in everything that happens with Charlotte… [She] touched something in me and I'm beyond anxious as to what will happen next after one heck of an explosive ending. — ***MJ Loves to Read***

A story of connection, passion, injustice, and secrets; a story of two lands caught up in oppression and strife, pulling the reader into a world where danger and desire burns freely, and where the protagonist's courage can cause both pain and pleasure. — ***Books, Tea, and Me***

PRAISE FOR *THE VIRTUES OF VICE*

Compulsive conclusion to *Ground Sweet as Sugar*. Vivid characters will remain with you after you close the pages. Fabulous fiction threaded through history, which has completely captured my curiosity. So richly written, feels like I've watched a movie rather than read a book. — *Review*

A page-turning conclusion to a grand saga! — ***For the Love of a Book***

The characters were in depth and complex... there wasn't a moment I was not in awe of their humanity and flaws. I kept ending up in research rabbit holes with each historical reference. This book was fascinating. Highly recommend! —*Review*

The Virtues of Vice is exactly the kind of conclusion I wanted for the *Ground Sweet as Sugar* duet. Catherine C. Heywood took all the puzzle pieces, jagged and otherwise, that were laid out before us and meticulously found their place... Wow. What a story. — ***MJ Loves to Read***

I read this book in less than a day, I didn't want to put it down. — *Review*

Heywood, as always provides a story that drags the reader into some wonderful escapism, romance and high drama. A book of consuming love, justice, power and revenge, where the end to all virtue is finally happiness. —***Books, Tea, and Me***

I didn't want the story to end. — *Review*

PRAISE FOR *MAY LEAVE STARS*

A vivid world… of the female and society's judgements and expectations. Of power, control, passion, troubles, and hardships. — ***Books, Tea, and Me***

Catherine C. Heywood's Paris burns hotter and shines brighter — her prose clever and banter sharp — making the reader feel as though they are walking through the city's streets. A story sure to capture your imagination and tug at your heart! — ***Author A.R. Hadley***

I loved Jasper and Amélie as a couple. Their chemistry was tangible… But it's the backdrop and setting that makes the intense romance stand out. — ***Raya's Reads***

This book was amazing. This is the way historical fiction should be done, with enough romance and drama to keep the reading going! Loved it! — ***Review***

I absolutely love [Heywood's] attention to detail and her historical research is so clear. She really makes the world of late-19th century Paris come to life. — ***Little But Fierce Book Diary***

Wow! What a fantastic book. I would give it more than 5 stars if I could… Not only did I care about the characters and the story was interesting and evolving, but I learned so much about Paris at the end of the 19th century. How laundresses were treated, assumptions made about female artists or entertainers, the intricate politics between women and their suitors… Still, at the heart of it is a love story between these two characters, which binds the reader's emotions and carries you through everything. I want to read more books by Catherine Heywood. — ***Review***

ALSO BY CATHERINE C. HEYWOOD

NOVELS
May Leave Stars
May Leave Stars: The Writer's Cut
Ground Sweet as Sugar
The Virtues of Vice

NOVELLAS
The California Limited
Girl in Bath

Into the Complete Unknown

CATHERINE C. HEYWOOD

MARAIS
media

Into the Complete Unknown is a work of fiction. Apart from the well-known names and locales that figure in the narrative, all names, characters, places, and incidents are the products of the author's imagination or are used fictitiously. Any resemblance to current events or locales, or to living persons, is entirely coincidental.

Copyright © 2021 by Catherine C. Heywood
Published by Marais Media, LLC
All rights reserved.

This book or parts thereof may not be reproduced in any form, stored in any retrieval system, or transmitted in any form by any means—electronic, mechanical, photocopy, recording, or otherwise—without prior written permission from the publisher. For permission requests, write to the author.

Grateful acknowledgement to Andrew Harvey for permission to reprint his translation of "Love is the Master" by Rumi.

Excerpt by Robert Emmet, from "Speech from the Dock," copyright © 1803, is in the public domain, distributed under the CC BY-SA 3.0 license.

ISBN: 978-1-951699-13-0

Cover Design and Formatting:
Qamber Designs & Media W.L.L.

Cover Images:
Rosina by John Singer Sargent, distributed under a CC0 1.0 license
Grapes by ONYXprj
Back image by lenisecalleja.photography

Author Image:
Jenny Loew Photography

Illustrations:
Joanna Pasek at Qamber Designs

Editors:
Kate Leibfried at Click Clack Writing
Devon Burke at Joy Editing

For the women who won't be eclipsed

GLOSSARY

artisan – in planter society, a slave or indentured servant highly valued as a skilled craftsman; she can rent out her skills and sell her goods and/or services at the market to earn her own money

cane piece – sugarcane field

hothouse – plantation hospital

pickney – Caribbean English for "child," derived from "pickaninny" but widely used without offensive connotation

Proty – rebel slang for "Protestant"

republican – in 18th century Ireland, someone who advocates for Ireland to become a republic, free of English sovereignty

tory – derived from the Irish Gaelic word *tóraidhe*, meaning outlaw; by the Cromwellian wars, a derogatory term for Irish Catholics dispossessed of land who became outlaws; later, often applied to any Irish Catholic or Royalist in arms

vigneron – a person who cultivates grapes for winemaking

*A note on St. Croix Creole – In writing the unique *patois* of St. Croix, my goal was to marry the accurate words and richness with reader accessibility. Where this falls short, it is entirely my own failing.

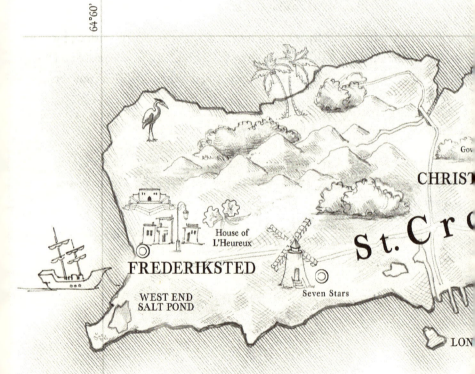

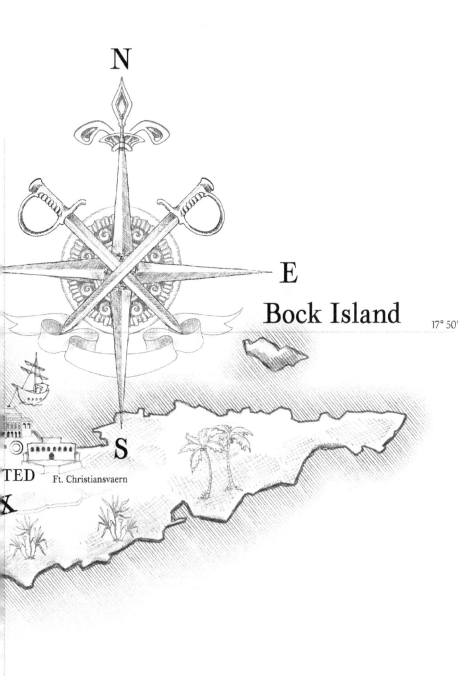

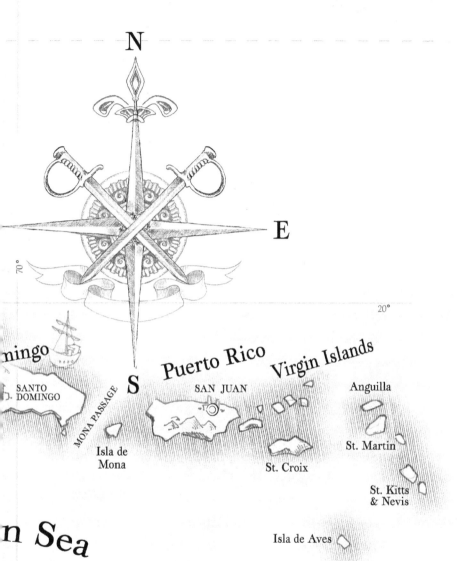

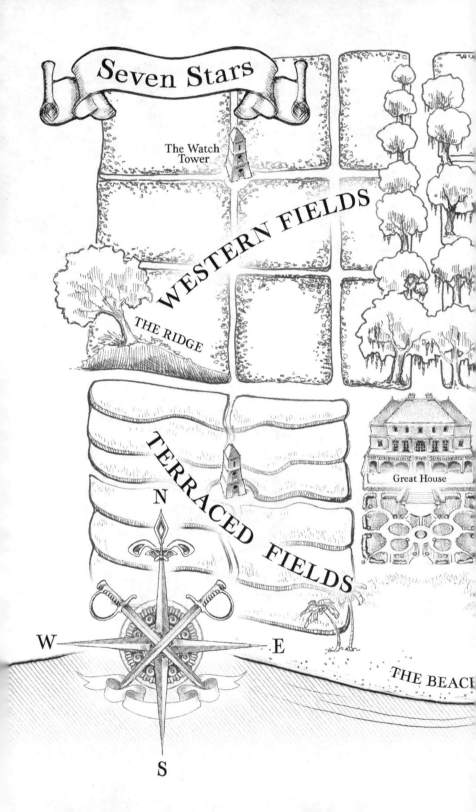

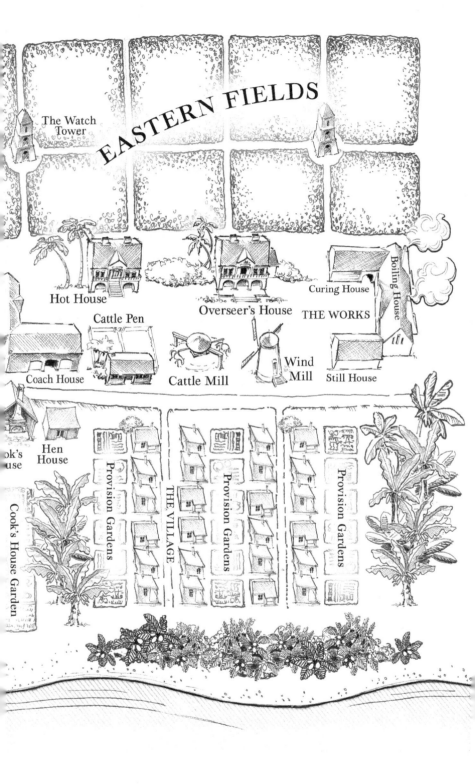

LOVE IS THE MASTER

Love is the One who masters all things;
I am mastered totally by Love.
By my passion of love for Love
I have ground sweet as sugar.
O furious Wind, I am only a straw before you;
How could I know where I will be blown next?
Whoever claims to have made a pact with Destiny
Reveals himself a liar and a fool;
What is any of us but a straw in a storm?
How could anyone make a pact with a hurricane?
God is working everywhere his massive Resurrection;
How can we pretend to act on our own?
In the hand of Love I am like a cat in a sack;
Sometimes Love hoists me into the air,
Sometimes Love flings me into the air,
Love swings me round and round His head;
I have no peace, in this world or any other.
The lovers of God have fallen in a furious river;
They have surrendered themselves to Love's commands.
Like mill wheels they turn, day and night, day and night,
Constantly turning and turning, and crying out.
—Rumi,
Translated by Andrew Harvey

*May you never forget what is worth remembering
nor ever remember what is best forgotten.*

—Irish Proverb

I

Mona Passage, Caribbean Sea
8th May, 1801

James Blair's first sense is a screaming pain in his head, as if his skull were shattered. The second is a rocking motion, as if the earth under him were bobbing back and forth. Third is a desperate thirst, as if his body has been starved of water for days. Lastly, he feels a soothing warmth on his face. He swallows and blinks, then peels his eyes open. The bright sun blinds him, and he drags an arm over his face.

"Captain, thank God!" a man says behind him.

James groans and tries to lift his large frame up, blinking again and again, urging his eyes to sift through the swirling kaleidoscope of sights for the plain truth—he sits on a lighter gliding along an aquamarine sea toward a sandy shore. His stomach churns as his mind churns, and he grips the edge of the lighter to steady himself. Still, the churning rises like a tide, and he hangs his head over the side and heaves a thin line of bile. James sighs, and his breaths come in pants. Everything—looking, sitting, breathing—feels like the most arduous chore while his head throbs and the world spins. Eventually, he turns, ever so slowly, to the earnest voice behind him—a young man, reed thin, his skin burnished by the sun, smiles with reassurance while he pulls oars through the water. Beyond the young man, James spies a sheared barque missing its foremast and mizzenmast.

"She's lame," the young man says, "but everything can be repaired."

James's eyes drift to the young man, and he nods. Then exhaustion overcomes him, and he lies back down, blissfully closing his eyes against the agony and confusion. How he knows the boat they glide in is called a lighter he can't say. For though he searches his memory, he hasn't a clue who the young man is rowing it.

Isla de Mona

The next time James wakes, the throbbing in his head is still merciless, but the earth under him is no longer bobbing. In the darkness, his mind and stomach are calm, so instead of opening his eyes, he drags a hand from his torso to glide along soft linen. He's no longer lying on a canvas cot but a feather bed. Exhaling slowly, he dares to open his eyes.

The light is shrouded, coming from a bank of windows at the stern, yet still James squeezes his eyes shut and groans. Bringing a shaky hand to his forehead, he tenderly cradles it, touching and testing. Piercing pain draws his searching fingertips around until he must lift his head from the pillow. There he feels a fine cloth sticking to his slick hair and, through it, a braid of sutures. For some reason, the ache in his head seems to grow now that he's discovered the source of it, and with a moan, he sinks back into his pillow and closes his eyes.

For a long time, James simply breathes in and out, grateful for the dark behind his lids, though his head feels full to bursting, like a thick sludge is pressing against every cavity and threatening to burst it. His heartbeat pulses in his ears along with a steady ringing. When both finally fade, he hears dull pounding and men calling, the scrape of a saw cutting through wood and the creak of straining rope. And he lies lame in bed.

Eventually, James braces himself and opens his eyes again. Wrought-iron lanterns, unlit for now, dangle from a wood-planked ceiling. Gingerly, he turns his head and ranges his gaze around the space—a wide desk and chair sit before the wall of windows, a large table that can sit six or more stands in the middle of the naked floor. For some reason, James knows that, but for the ornate scrollwork carved into the window frames, the captain's cabin is devoid of its majesty, as if it had been plundered.

Perhaps that was what happened, he muses. They met a privateer, and in the battle, he and the ship were devastated. Why, he wonders, can't he remember?

When more sounds of men working pierce through the mire of his thoughts, James groans and pulls himself to sitting, but again his sight and stomach spin. Closing his eyes, he cups his forehead and curses.

The next time James wakes, he spies a glass filled with a cloudy white liquid and swallows. Sitting up, he waits through the inevitable spinning that fades faster than it did before. He swings his long legs over the bedside and peers at his bare feet. Then he examines his hands and arms and torso. They all appear unhurt.

James stands on legs as limp as a newborn colt's and, for a long moment, simply stares at the glass while he steadies himself. When his feet are finally fixed under him, he staggers the few paces to the table and grips the glass, downing the sweet, crisp coconut milk in three grateful gulps.

Once again James studies the cabin. The young man called him a captain, and it rang true. This is a captain's cabin, yet somehow it appears foreign to him. He peers down again at his body, which feels perfectly familiar and, but for the obvious injury to his head, appears to be sound.

Just then, the young man enters and stops. "I'm sorry, Captain Blair. I should've knocked. I…" Chagrined, he looks back at the door. "It's just that you've been sleeping for so many days, I…"

"It's all right," James says, thinking. The young man's name still eludes him, and eventually he staggers back to the bed and slides in with a sigh.

"I can't tell you how glad I am to see you up." The young man's eyes fix on the empty glass. "And drinking. You gave us all quite a scare with your fall."

Fall? James desperately searches his dense mind for a memory he can retrieve of a fall. Yet after a long moment, he concedes there's nothing. "I have been sleeping."

"How is your head?" the young man asks, approaching the bed.

Thick, faulty, heavy, unforgiving. James could say all these, but he won't. "More agonizing than any pain I have ever felt."

The young man spies James looking at the empty glass and excuses himself to get more. When he returns, he hands another full glass to James, then takes a seat beside the bed. "I must admit," the young man looks down, abashed, "I thought you mad climbing that mast in the midst of a hurricane. But cutting the shrouds… you saved us, sir."

Once again, James's mouth falls open to speak. *Climbing the mast?* He can't fathom he'd do such a thing. While this man's name escapes him along with any memory of going through a hurricane, he does remember an earlier time. He's always had a deathly fear of heights.

"A hurricane," James says.

"I would not have believed it," the young man says, "so early in the season, had I not gone through it myself. But we're seeing to her repairs, and we'll give chase just as soon as we can."

"Give chase?" The words spill out before James can check them.

The young man frowns, his gaze scrutinizing his captain for a long moment. Eventually, he says, "I'm keeping you awake, sir. You suffered a tremendous injury to your head. I suppose it's only natural you be troubled with confusion. Rest more and I'll return later with something for you to eat."

Sometime later, James wakes to the sound of a tray sliding onto a table. Deep shadows play around the edges of the cabin, and the lanterns and some candelabras are now lit.

"The finest Mona has to offer," the young man says, indicating the tray filled with a pitcher of coconut water and plates bearing fruit and fish. "I know it isn't much, but it should hold us until we can set sail for Hispaniola."

"Mona," James says. This island he remembers. If only he could ask the young man his name without seeming completely enfeebled. "How long have we been here?"

"Some five days." The young man studies Captain Blair.

James drags himself to the table and sits across from the young man. After swallowing an entire glass of coconut water, he eyes the food. For the first time in days, he's not plagued by nausea, instead he feels a gnawing hunger and begins to eat. "How long do you imagine we should be here?"

"I can't say. The repairs are coming along, yet the problem is that we need to find not one but two tree trunks sturdy enough from which to fashion masts. We're lame without them."

James nods. "And Hispaniola?"

Again the young man looks at his captain speculatively, a growing unease showing on his face. Finally, he says, "You do know why we go to Hispaniola, don't you, sir?"

James searches his mind, but some memories prove as slippery as eels. Embarrassed, he sighs and smiles with feigned amusement. "I'm afraid I can't recall," he finally utters.

The young man's mouth falls open and for an unbearable moment to James, he simply stares. "You don't know why we were going to Hispaniola? But you know your indenture, Charlotte Dillon, right? Surely, you remember her, sir."

"Charlotte Dillon? I don't know that name."

More than three weeks pass, and with each day, James's headaches, nausea, and confusion fade. After the young man's shock, he sets about filling in the gaps in his captain's memory. He tells him of his plantation, Seven Stars, which James recalls, and of his merchant shipping fleet, which he doesn't. Filling in these gaps begins to root him in this time and place. Yet the young man—who James learns is named Tim Rogers and has been a member of his shipping crews for five years—he still cannot recall. Nor, apparently, the entire reason for this folly. A woman, his indenture, by the name of Charlotte Dillon. A runaway. It seems James had some feelings of affection for her strong enough to give chase. Still, no matter how much he searches the holes in his mind for her, there are only bottomless wells of nothing.

In early June, James is leaning against a railing on the main deck, staring at the blood-red sun as it slips into the Caribbean Sea, when Tim approaches. "West or east, Captain?"

The first mate told James everything he knew about Charlotte. That she was an Irish convict who signed a seven-year indenture. That she was quick-witted and beautiful. That they had a stormy friendship. That she was kidnapped and turned privateer for two years. That she and her crew pillaged James's own ships, thieving and murdering, but that when she was returned to James, they had an affair. By all accounts, a true love affair.

Still, out of all the things Tim has told James, most of it dusting off its rightful place inside his mind, this account, this most significant woman, yields a stubborn blank. Now, on the eve of their departure, he's faced with a decision only he can make.

"West?" James turns to Tim, who nods. "In good wind, we should reach the port in…"

"Three days," Tim supplies. "Four, at most."

James nods, lost in trying to remember.

"You won't regret it, sir. I promise you. You're remembering more and more each day. You're bound to remember her soon enough. And when you do, we'll be there to confront the *Joyeuse* for helping her to escape."

James nods and strolls back to his cabin for the night. But a half hour later, when he's finally lying in bed, his head and heart pounding, he curses the great gap in his mind. With the possible exception of being quick-witted and beautiful, nothing in the first mate's account of Charlotte Dillon sounds like a woman James would love. How, he wonders, could he excuse such behavior of hers? How could he thrust himself and a ship full of men into a storm to chase after her? The only explanation could be love. Yet the harder James pushes, the further away he feels from remembering, as if he's grasping at the mist.

Marigot, St. Martin

Charlotte Dillon is locked in an embrace of steel with Nico Bautista. They exchange a sly smile, then she pulls away, the edge of her cutlass scraping against his.

"Had enough?" he taunts before taking a sip from his pouch. "You look winded," he says, offering the leather bag, which she takes.

After drinking, Charlotte throws her heavy, red braid over her shoulder and sighs. At four months, she no longer suffers nausea, and her energy has fully returned. Her belly is noticeably rounding now against her small frame. Still, it isn't large. But in truth, she can't draw as deep a breath as she could even a month ago.

"I'm fine," she says, assuming her fighting stance once more and pointing her blade at his chest.

Again they spar, a dance of thrusts and parries, scrapes and clangs, until there's a gasp.

"What *are* you doing?" Luci Bautista says, stalking out to the back garden and taking the blade from her husband. "You would fight a woman *enceinte*? Are you mad?"

"She insisted," he says.

"Really," Charlotte says. "I'm feeling so vital these days, I thought—"

"And you must obey everything she suggests?" Luci says, crowding menacingly in her husband's face. "One careless moment, one slip of the blade, and you've run her and the babe through. You do not think, Nico."

"I promise it's all right," Charlotte says.

"I'm merely keeping her sharp since she insists on leaving us," Nico says, caressing Luci's waist.

She slaps his hand away and turns back for the door, muttering about fools and France.

Port of Santo Domingo, Santo Domingo, Hispaniola

Four days later, the *Amity* finally trundles into the port of Santo Domingo. There, James follows Tim to the port authority.

"The *Joyeuse*?" the first mate asks.

"Long gone."

"What do you mean?" Tim asks. "Surely she went through the same storm we did."

"Sure enough and suffered some good damage, too. But her luck, she was buffeted neatly into our port, saw to her repairs, and set off for Jamaica after only two weeks."

"She's gone," James utters.

"Yes, sir. But I expect her back this way soon."

Tim and James exchange a measuring look, then stroll back to the ship. The first mate insists that missing the *Joyeuse* is not the setback it appears. That they must wait regardless. That they need to make better, more lasting repairs to the *Amity*. But James scarcely hears any of it while his head pounds and his belly roils.

Ten days pass while they make more repairs to the *Amity*, until finally the *Joyeuse* pulls into the port. James and Tim wait on the dock for the captain to disembark, and when a sailor thumbs a short, stocky man with a laurel of white hair strolling down the gangplank, James steps before him. "Good day, Captain. I have some reason to believe you may have given aid to someone for whom I am searching."

Captain Daniels stops. "Oh?"

"Did you pick up a woman on St. Croix nearly two months ago?"

"No."

Captain Daniels moves to stride past them, but Tim looks frantically at James's calm and grabs the captain's arm.

"Search your mind, sir," Tim says.

The captain looks askance at Tim's grasp, then raises a piqued brow.

Tim looks imploringly to James, then continues. "She has long, red hair, is medium height. Her name is Charlotte Dillon, and she's a bondswoman fleeing an indenture. We must have her back."

"Sir"—Daniels wrenches his arm from Tim—"I didn't pick up a woman on St. Croix because I've never picked up a woman. They're bad luck on ships, and I've made it a practice never to entertain such a notion."

"I thank you, Captain," James says, turning away.

Yet Tim darts in front of the captain, blocking his way. "She may've been dressed as a man."

James regards Tim with astonishment. "The man claims he doesn't have her. What nonsense is this about dressing as a man?"

"Young man," Captain Daniels says, "I didn't pick up anyone on my last visit to St. Croix. No one."

"There. You see?" James says.

Tim sighs. "Captain, this woman is not simply a bondswoman. She means a great deal to this man." He indicates James. "A great deal."

Captain Daniels regards James, who appears to be completely unmoved, then frowns, disconcerted.

"If she's persuaded you to protect her from us," Tim continues, "to hide her… We simply must have her back."

Now it's Captain Daniels's turn to sigh and regard Tim with exasperation. "I swear to you on the continued good health of my family, I did *not* pick up this woman you seek. Not dressed as a woman, nor dressed as a man. No one. I picked up no one. I can see you're distressed." Again he peers, confused, at James. "But I assure you, I had nothing whatsoever to do with the disappearance of this woman you seek. On my honor, young man, I *swear it*."

"There you have it, Tim," James says. To the captain, he says, "I'm sorry for taking up so much of your time." He doffs his hat. "Good day—"

"But… she has to be," Tim rasps desperately. "Yours was the only ship that left the island that morning."

"I think you're wrong."

"Pardon me?"

"A mail packet was docking as we weighed anchor."

Back in the *Amity's* captain's cabin, James slams the door and glares at Tim. "You made me look like a fool. I should sack you this very instant. How you went on and on, despite the man's denials. 'Dressed as a man.' What absurdity! Are you quite certain it isn't you who has feelings for this woman? Because that's exactly what the good captain was himself thinking. I can guarantee you that."

"I'll not apologize," Tim says. "You can sack me, but I'll not be sorry for doing the one thing we set out to do when we left St. Croix on first May. If we didn't press the captain, all we sacrificed in the storm would be for naught. Keogh would have my head."

John Keogh, James's dearest friend, he remembers, too. The name alone was like a magical lock that opened more doors behind which James's memories lay.

"Now we have another clue," the first mate continues. "The mail packet. It's ingenious, really. And if we set a good pace for home, perhaps we can meet it on first July. It should hold the answers you seek. Surely."

"We are going home. As to the mail packet, I don't care."

"Pardon me?"

"I have a plantation to return to. People, real people, who reside in my mind and heart to return to. I cannot make a life out of chasing the ghost of this woman."

"But—"

"If she is as important to me as you say, my memories of her will return. Until then, I must gather the pieces of my life that are familiar. I don't expect you to understand what it is to search one's mind and find gaps. I do, however, expect you to obey me, as your captain. This Charlotte Dillon can wait."

Tim's mouth falls open, and he shakes his head. He wants desperately to object but fears the very real ramifications of pressing. Finally, he decides there's no help for it. "You shall lose her, sir. If you stop searching, you'll lose her, and you may never get her back."

James shrugs. "She's already lost to me."

2

Port of Christiansted, Christiansted, St. Croix

Though Tim harried him on the return journey to go faster to meet the mail packet, nothing the young man could say would sway James. On the second of July, the *Amity* eventually grinds into Gallows Bay. While she docks, James scans the port lanes and fort with relief. Perhaps he could admit there was something of fear in his slow-paced return, fear that he would return home and not remember it. Yet he recognizes it all.

"Ah, Christ," Keogh says when James disembarks, "you look like shite."

In truth, he does. James's honey-blonde hair has grown shaggy, and he's grown a full beard. His indigo-blue eyes have deep circles under them, and he's lost some weight on his broad six-and-a-half-foot frame.

But for James, gripped by a relief so strong that he recognizes his dearest friend, his throat tightens, and his eyes grow wet while he throws his arms around Keogh, then rubs the man's sun-burnished bald head.

"Here now," the big man says, patting James on the back. "What's all this? You missed your old mate so much?" When James merely hugs his friend tighter, Keogh adds, "Perhaps I should welcome you with more insults."

At Keogh's house, the man hands James a heavy pour of rum. "We know where she is, Jamie."

James eyes another man who accompanied them, then falls onto a settee and takes a sip of rum. "Charlotte Dillon," he says, staring into his glass.

Keogh exchanges a confused glance with the other man, then says, "Yes. Charlotte."

James nods.

"I'm sorry you missed the mail packet," Keogh continues. "The captain confirmed she secured passage on the cutter and headed east. He saw her safely to St. Martin."

Again, James nods.

Keogh and the other man exchange another confused look, then the big man takes a seat and smooths his muttonchops. "I understand you were caught in the storm. Tim told me the *Amity* and her crew barely survived. Would not have if not for your cleverness and courage."

"That's what I was told, too." James meets Keogh's gaze. "But I don't remember." He shrugs. "I've no memory of the storm at all. No memory of the chase that preceded it. No memory whatever of some time, it seems."

Keogh's and the other man's mouths fall open. For a long moment, there's only the *tick, tick, ticking* of a clock.

Eventually, James peers at the other man. As he came to do with Tim and the others on the *Amity*, he studies the man with chestnut-brown curls, steel-blue eyes, and an arrow nose for any flicker of recognition he can urge to light. Finally, James curses himself and says, "I should know you?"

"Y-yes, sir. I run your shipping office. I served my indenture at Seven Stars. As a driver."

"Your best driver," Keogh interjects.

"My name is Darcy Shea."

They shake hands, and James says, "Mr. Shea."

"Just Shea, if you please. You call me Shea."

James nods and drags his fingertips across his forehead, a recent tic he's developed as if to urge the brain tucked behind it to work.

"I remember my boyhood and sailing," James says. "I remember discovering sugar planting and St. Croix. I remember purchasing Jane's Hope and freeing my slaves. But…"

When James fails to go on, Keogh prompts, "Then you turned to indentures. Do you remember that?"

"I remember deciding on it, but..."

"Shea was in your first class, and he's first among them. You hold him in high regard. *We* hold him in high regard."

Again, James stares at the man called Shea, a man he should know and yet doesn't. "Then I must thank you," he says.

Keogh and Shea exchange a knowing look. Now Shea is even more racked with guilt for his role in Charlotte's escape.

"So, you'll sail to St. Martin, then," Keogh says. "The trail leads there. We can make the *Amity* ready within a matter hours."

James takes another drink and shakes his head. "I'll not be leaving for St. Martin."

"Well, of course. Not today," the big man says. "Take the night here. Rest up. Twelve hours will make little difference at this point."

"You don't understand," James says. "I don't intend to go to St. Martin because I don't intend to keep chasing this Charlotte Dillon."

"What?" Keogh says in breathless astonishment. "Jamie, you have to go. You risked Miss Lund's threats, your life, your crew's lives. You love this woman. Don't tell me you don't remember *her*."

James peers dolefully at Keogh, then shakes his head.

Keogh and Shea exchange a look of astonishment.

"You must remember her," Shea says.

"I must?"

"Jamie," the big man says, "she carries your child."

Now it's James's turn to look at Keogh in astonishment.

"My child," James utters. "Are you certain?"

"I suppose Tim didn't tell you that because he didn't know. Yes. Your child. After Charlotte fled, I tried to convince you to let her go. After all, you were set to say goodbye to her. You were marrying Miss Lund and—"

"Marrying Miss Lund?" James says. The image that blooms in the man's mind is of a knobby-kneed girl. "The governor-general's blonde pickney?"

"She's not some girl anymore, Jamie. Jenny Lund has grown into a fetching young woman. You don't remember?"

James glares at Keogh, downs his rum, and stands to leave. But the big man blocks him.

"I-I'm sorry. This is a lot to take in. I'm sorry. I just... I don't know what to say. This woman means the world to you."

"Which woman?"

"Charlotte," Shea says, his tone sharp. Between the two of them, it seems that James is always carelessly moving on while Shea is always entrusted with keeping the memory of her. And now, even though he knows that James has suffered a grievous injury to his head, the younger man feels angry. "You love her, and she loves you. Believe me, I wish that were not true because I loved her once, but she chose you. She will always choose you."

James stares open-mouthed at Shea. When he looks to Keogh, the big man nods.

"And Miss Lund?" James asks.

"Is a complication," Keogh replies. "A serious one, but..."

"And she's here? At the governor-general's residence? This fetching young woman who's to be my wife? Meanwhile, I'm chasing after another woman who was not to be my wife but who, nevertheless, carries my child? Is that about the state of things?"

"Those are the bare facts, but—"

James's cheeks flood a vivid red. "I don't remember the man who made those decisions. Frankly, I'm not sure I want to remember him. He sounds like a lecher, a cad, a thief."

"No, Jamie. Don't do this to yourself while your mind is still addled. When you find Charlotte, you'll remember."

"Like I remembered Mr. Shea here?"

Keogh looks at Shea. "Shea was a good driver when we needed one. A fine man. Even, in some ways, your friend today. But the feelings you have for him, the feelings you have for me, for that matter, pale in comparison to what you feel for her."

James shakes his head, and Keogh nods. They sit in this silent stalemate for a long moment until, eventually, James says, "And this Charlotte Dillon is *perhaps* on St. Martin?"

"Perhaps," Keogh says. "A week's sail east."

"A week's sail east and I *may* find her. Just like when Tim told me we needed to sail west to Hispaniola. That we'd find her there. And when we didn't, he told me we must wait for the *Joyeuse*. That we'd find her then, and we didn't. Has it not occurred to any of you, because it's certainly occurred to me, that this Charlotte clearly doesn't want to be found?"

At length, James and Keogh and Shea regard each other.

Eventually, Keogh says, "You don't need to decide right away."

"I have decided."

"Sleep on it, Jamie. There's no harm in giving yourself a little more time to decide. Now you know she's carrying your child. Perhaps you don't owe anything to Charlotte, but you owe something to your child."

After Shea leaves, Keogh fills in the gaps in James's memory. Weary, James closes his eyes and listens to his friend tell him the story of his life over the past eight years. All about James's love for sugar planting, how successful his transition to indentures has been, how the plantation has grown, how he's won the yields, how he met Charlotte. He tells him every detail he can through when Charlotte was kidnapped.

"That's when I courted Miss Lund?" Again, James searches his mind through the handful of memories he has of Jenny. He can acknowledge perhaps there was some potential there. After all, she had fetching features and a plucky personality.

"At my insistence, I'm afraid," Keogh says. "I worried you still grieved Charlotte."

Keogh tells James of the attacks on James's ships, how they destroyed the pirate crew and reclaimed Charlotte, that James punished her but not as severely as she deserved.

"Because I loved her," James supplies.

"Because you love her."

Again, James sighs.

"And that's when you began an affair with Charlotte in earnest. It was brief because Miss Lund found out and threatened you."

"I can't say that I blame her." James pauses in contemplation, trying desperately to square his behavior with his beliefs about himself, his beliefs about what a good man does and doesn't do. "Do I care about this Miss Lund at all?"

"I don't know. I thought you well suited once, but now… I just don't know."

"This picture of James Blair that you paint—the James Blair that loves Charlotte Dillon—he sounds unmoored, irrational, careless. How could I—?"

"Alive. At no time since I've known you have you been so alive as you were with her."

"Even though we fought?"

"Especially because you fought. The first words you exchanged with her were challenges, and the contests never stopped. I don't believe you'd ever met a woman who stood up to you in such a fashion, and you need that."

James and Keogh exchange a sardonic grin.

"I'm tired," James says. "This injury still makes me sleep, at times, like a babe."

When James stands to find a bed, the big man says, "I'm glad you're back."

"Not all the way."

"You'll get there. I've no doubt."

Yet when James crawls into bed, he can't help but lie awake, sinking all the seeds of information he's been given and praying they bear fruit in the gaps in his mind. Nearly all that Keogh shared of him feels intrinsically true—James's commitment, despite the scorn of slaveholding planters, to indentures, his instincts and success in sugar and shipping, even his courting of Miss Lund. All this sounds like the man he was becoming, a man he would be proud to be.

All except for Charlotte Dillon. Still, when he falls asleep, his last thoughts are of her.

Why can't I remember you?

The next morning, James confronts Keogh as he prepares to leave.

"Where do you go?" Keogh asks.

"The governor-general's residence."

"I'm afraid you'll not find a warm welcome. You were supposed to be married tomorrow."

"Tomorrow?"

"Of course, all the plans were abandoned when you left." Keogh pauses, considering. "Will you tell her of the gaps in your memory?"

"I don't know."

"She might be more forgiving if you did."

"Do I want her to forgive me? Do you?"

"I don't know. What I do know is that I don't want her to carry out her threat against Charlotte. You may not remember that she carries your child, but I do. I wouldn't see either of them hurt."

"What of this threat against Charlotte?"

Keogh explains about the letters James wrote to the Crown in a fit of anger, about the one letter Jenny discovered that details Charlotte's pirating and suggests she's a wanted murderer.

"But she hasn't sent it?" James asks.

Keogh shakes his head.

"You're certain?"

"As certain as I can be."

"Then I must bear up and see her."

While James walks out the door, Keogh says, "Whatever you do, just promise me you won't forget about Charlotte."

James chortles. "I can't forget what I can't remember."

3

Governor-General's Residence

After enduring a half-hour harangue from the governor-general and his wife on the deficiencies of his character, James is reluctantly allowed out to the garden to see their daughter. Strolling along the walkways, into the heady scents of warm honey and citrus, James can't help but feel an eerie sense of slipping through time, marveling at how the trees and shrubs, vines and flowers, have grown since last he remembers them.

Near the fountain, James slows, spying a young woman standing in a high-waisted white gown, her head down and her golden-blonde hair styled up.

"Miss Lund?"

Jenny looks up and fixes her molten-brown eyes on James. His heart starts to thud, and his breath leaves him. Though he tries, James can scarcely see the little girl he remembers in this alluring woman.

"You're so beautiful."

Beside the fountain, Jenny is disarmed. James wears the most peculiar look of wonder on his face, a look so similar to the one he wore when they locked eyes at her debut all those years ago now that she's immediately thrust back there. Then she's reminded of the terrible predicament he left her in. "And you, Mr. Blair, are a miserable excuse for a man," she says. But the hostile edge is gone.

"Yes," he admits.

James smiles shyly and takes a step toward Jenny, and the vulnerability in his bearing and voice makes her so unnerved she steps back.

"Did you find her?" she asks. "The slut for whom you broke our engagement? Did you?"

The acid in Jenny's voice wrenches James from his stupor. This is no persuadable maiden but a woman scorned.

"You're upset and have every right to be. I treated you horribly, and for that I am sorry."

"Sorry?"

James nods.

"You return the day before we were to be married with some gilded words and, what? Am I to forgive you? Take you back?"

"I don't know."

And in truth, he doesn't. James only knew he had to see Miss Lund, and now that he has, he finds he wants to see more of her.

"Where is she?" Jenny asks.

"I don't know."

"You've lost her, then. So, you've come groveling back to me. Will you continue looking for her?"

"I don't know."

"You don't know where she is or if you'll go on searching. You don't know why you're here. What do you know?"

"I know that I'm sorry."

At length, James and Jenny stare at each other until she finally says, "Go away, Jamie."

He nods and turns to leave, then stops. "The letter. Might I see it?"

Jenny chortles. "Of course, *that* is why you came. I can't let you see it because I don't have it."

James turns back to her. "You don't have it?"

"I mailed it."

"You didn't."

"Your dogs weren't nipping at my heels every minute of every day." Jenny smiles tightly. She's imagined this day many times, when James would return begging for knowledge about the letter. Each time, she imagined feeling triumphant. But now, Jenny can't say what it is about James that makes her feel so unsatisfied—his pale demeanor, perhaps—only that she is unsatisfied. "I mailed it. Now we wait and see what happens."

Seven Stars

As the carriage turns under the canopy of mahogany and moss, Keogh clears his throat, and James opens his eyes. Peering into the distance, he glimpses the familiar gray-and-rose stone great house. A short time later, the carriage pulls to a stop in the courtyard, and James looks around, spying O'Neil and Celine awaiting him. When he gets out, he's greeted just as he remembers and nods with a tremulous smile. Then he peers down the limestone lane to a village that has doubled in size since he last remembers.

"Time enough for a tour tomorrow," Keogh says, urging him up the stairs.

Over the days that follow, Keogh and James explore the plantation—from the village where they examine the new houses and talk to some of the indentures, to the works where they stroll the aisles between cones and vats, routinely stopping to chat about best practices over the years. They trot down every cane break, stop at every cane piece, and discuss every variety of cane. While they ride in the plantation's seams, the seams in James's own mind knit together. This, he knows, is home. And with that sure knowledge comes his confidence. Until they reach the hothouse. There he spies the head nurse. The former slave has walnut skin and a long fall of black braids twisted into one great one.

"Juneh." James gives her a soft smile. "I was hoping you would still be here."

"Wheh I go, Masteh Blaih? Hm? Wha' you do wit'out me?"

"What would I do, indeed." James looks around at the beds, then back to the nurse. "I'm told you're keeping a masterful hold on this hothouse. That it's a premier one on the island."

"Yes, sir." Juneh glances fearfully at Keogh. She'd heard the rumors, that the planter had returned with part of his mind missing, but didn't want to credit them. "You didn't find her?"

"Juneh and Charlotte shared a room," Keogh explains.

James nods absently. "No." After a pause, he says, "I wonder, perhaps she doesn't want me to find her. Maybe it would be best to leave her be."

Again, Juneh looks at Keogh, then at James. "You got my note, sir?"

"You'll have to forgive him, Juneh," the big man says. "Master Blair suffered a grievous injury to his head in a storm. I'm afraid it's rendered some of his memory compromised."

James glares at Keogh. "Must you do this? Make excuses for me with absolutely everyone we meet?"

"Not everyone," Keogh insists. "But your artisans have a right to know. And in particular, given her friendship with Charlotte, Juneh should know." The big man looks to the nurse. "He got your note. He'd all but given up on retrieving Charlotte until he saw your words. I can't say I thank you for that."

"He had a right to know about his child," Juneh says. "I's not sorry. I told her oveh and oveh again to tell him, but she refuse. Somet'ing about an old love of Masteh Blaih's who pled her belly." The nurse looks at him. "You really not find her? Foh true?"

"No," James says.

"Not yet," Keogh says at the same time.

James glares at Keogh, and the big man glares right back.

"I thank you for your diligence with the hothouse, Juneh." And with that, James turns to leave.

"Jamie, you should talk to Juneh about Charlotte."

From the doorway, James sighs. "Perhaps I shall. Not today."

After a long moment, Keogh utters under his breath to Juneh, "I'll be back." Then he follows James out the door.

At the stable, Keogh catches up with James while they turn their horses over to the groom, but before he can speak, James says, "Don't mistake this for ungratefulness, but I think it's time you return to Christiansted."

"Oh no," Keogh says, "you sound positively overwhelmed with gratitude."

They exchange an eye roll.

"I am," James says. "Truly. I can't tell you how many times I've tried to imagine resuming my life here without your knowledge to fill in the gaps. But I've had you and Tim shadowing me since I woke from my injury, stepping in and interceding and explaining. I'm home now, and it feels like home. It's time that I make it on my own."

Later that afternoon, while James is engrossed in studying his paperwork from his overseer, Keogh returns to the hothouse to find Juneh.

"May we speak privately?"

"Yes, sir."

Juneh flags another nurse, Sisi, to attend to her patient, then strides out to the deserted veranda. While the sugar works thrum in the distance, the former overseer and the nurse look out over the eastern fields.

"You eveh miss being heh?" Juneh finally asks.

"Not until now," Keogh replies.

"Why now?"

"You can see—more than anyone on this plantation, I suspect—that Master Blair is lost."

Juneh looks down and shakes her head. "I neveh t'ought I see de day he forget about her."

"Nor I. So, you see why I'm concerned."

"Yes, sir. I do."

"Can you help him?"

The nurse shakes her head. "I can't say I knows anyt'ing about a lost mind. Not de propeh herbs."

"But you know the spells," Keogh utters.

Juneh looks at Keogh with quelling eyes, then quickly looks around them and shakes her head.

"You do."

"I don't know what you mean, sir."

"You're a conjurer. I don't care if it's healing plants or magic from the moon. I would enlist anything to help him recover what he's lost. You know what he's lost."

At length, Juneh stares at Keogh, then finally she shakes her head. "I make no promises."

"I'm leaving tomorrow morning. I just… I just want to know someone is trying to help him. Even if it doesn't work."

Over the days that follow, Juneh enlists the help of a light-fingered domestic and slowly gathers what she'll need for the spell. When storm clouds gather and the skies open up, the nurse races through the rain to the windmill. Inside, Juneh reverently builds her altar. First, she creates a wide circle of candles and lights them. In the center, she places a bowl of herbs, a jar of honey, the candle from the hurricane lamp she shared with Charlotte, a piece of parchment, a quill and inkwell, a string of yarn, a queen chess piece from James's set—Charlotte had told her she and James used to play—a linen pillowcase from James's bed, Charlotte's hair brush that she left behind, a lock of James's hair lifted from his own brush, a silver buckle from James's wardrobe, and seven coins.

When all the pieces are nestled neatly around the center candle, Juneh entwines ropes of beads around her neck and sits, crossing her legs. Then she anoints the center candle with honey and rolls it through the herbs. Centering the sweetened candle, Juneh lights it and closes her eyes, relaxes her body, and lets her mind drift. First, she imagines Charlotte, then James, their faces, their voices. And while wind howls, rain pelts, and thunder cracks, Juneh holds her hands over the flame and begins to chant:

"Fill your daughteh Charlotte wit' love. Fill your son James wit' love."

Meanwhile, up the path to the great house, James, sleeping soundly, begins to stir.

In the windmill, Juneh continues. "Whispeh to her. Whispeh to him."

In bed, James's mouth falls open, his breathing grows heavy, and his eyes bounce under their lids.

James can hear voices shouting at him, but he can't make out the words. He can see giant waves breaking over him, but he can't escape the deluge. He's battered and tossed…

In the windmill, Juneh opens her arms and raises her voice, matching the thunder outside with a thunder from her chest. "Fill your daughteh Charlotte wit' love. Fill your son James wit' love. Whispeh to her. Whispeh to him." Juneh chants it over and over while, in his bed, James pants and squirms. Finally, Juneh pulls her palms together before her and says, "Equally to de sout', to de nort', to de west, and to de east. Let her belong to him and he to her. Fill him wit' remembering."

Next Juneh writes James's and Charlotte's names on the piece of parchment and drips wax from the burning candle over them until the names are covered. While the wax is hardening, she presses their hair to it. Then she rolls up the parchment and ties it with the yarn. Eventually, she blows the candle out.

In his bed, James suddenly falls still on his back with his arms splayed wide.

James drifts through a murky, azure sea. A muffled woman's voice, like an echo, sounds from somewhere far above. He looks up to see jeweled facets of waves dancing under a brilliant sun, and only then does he realize he's submerged. But he isn't breathless, isn't swimming, isn't desperate to crest the surface at all. In fact, when the voice sounds again, he looks up and discovers he's even farther away. He's floating down, down, down. But that voice… even as it fades, it is all that is tranquil in the tempest.

James opens his eyes to a midnight dark. Outside, a storm rages, but safe in his bed, he feels a serenity in his soul he hasn't felt since waking from his injury. Training his gaze into the shadows, he tries to make sense of the peculiar dream. Even though he was storm-tossed and then it appeared he was falling, perhaps even drowning, after some moments, he determines still he doesn't feel frightened or concerned, only intrigued. So, James turns over and closes his eyes, eager to return to the siren.

Marigot, St. Martin

Meanwhile, in her *alcoba*, Charlotte wakes feeling a pang in her heart she hasn't felt in some weeks. Her eyes well with tears, and the baby moves inside her. Charlotte slides a hand to her belly and tenderly rubs it. Then, knuckling her tears away, she turns over and goes back to sleep.

4

The next morning, Charlotte demurs when it's time to leave for mass.

"I'll catch up to you," she tells Luci. "I must stop at the bank."

But instead of going to the bank, Charlotte veers off for the port. The night before, she woke feeling the strongest pull to James, as if he were very near to her. In truth, as if he were inside her, every part of her. Her heart ached terribly, and when she woke this morning still feeling the same throbbing in her chest, she knew she had to do something.

At the docks, Charlotte scans the ships and spies a man-of-war with a gleaming tricolor ensign waving in the breeze. Breathless with hope, she strides to the gangplank and boards. On the main deck, a young sailor heaving a barrel spies her. With a grunt, he lets his load go, wipes his brow, and says in a thick French accent, "Madam?"

"May I please speak with your captain, sir?" she replies in French. "It's urgent."

In the captain's cabin, she's introduced to Gabriel Rainier, a trim man of middling years with a cocksure gaze.

The captain invites her to sit, resumes his chair, then clasps his hands together. "Madam?"

"Are you shortly returning to France?" Charlotte asks in French.

"Tomorrow," Rainier says.

Charlotte exhales. "Might I secure passage?" When Rainier begins to shake his head, she continues. "Captain, I must sail to France as soon as possible." She strokes her burgeoning belly, and the captain regards it as if only now noticing she's pregnant. He narrows his gaze.

"My life and the life of my babe are imperiled here. I'm afraid I'm being chased by a murderous madman. He…" Charlotte summons tears. "He will kill us, sir. You alone have the power to prevent it."

Captain Rainier squirms in his chair and clears his throat. "Where is this madman now? Do you need my protection this very moment?"

"Sailing to St. Martin as we speak. To arrive in only a matter of days, I'm told. Two, three at the most. I'm safe for now, but I must get myself and my baby off this island as soon as possible."

"Hmm," the captain says. "Yes."

"So, you'll help me?"

"If I might ask, when is your little one…" The captain waves his fingers at Charlotte's belly while the scandalous words catch on his tongue.

"Due? Not for some months. If we leave tomorrow and sail straight for France, I should be there well before his time."

"Hmm," the captain says again. It's a delicate business, a woman *enceinte*. But his chivalry will not allow him to turn her away. Reluctantly, the man nods and says, "Of course, I shall help you, madam."

With her passage secure, Charlotte strides to the back garden chapel, slips in, and kneels beside Luci, who smiles unsuspectingly. Then she bends her head and sends a prayer of gratitude to the heavens.

That night, Charlotte lies awake, thinking of the Caribbean. That first jeweled glimpse of St. Croix. The unique spices and foods. The melody of Creole. All of it she'll miss more than she imagined when she first arrived.

But inevitably, Charlotte's thoughts return to James. She recalls Nico's words urging her to tell James of her pregnancy. How reasonable they sounded. Yet she knows that James, no matter his feelings or hers, cannot marry a convict-cum-pirate. She loves him, and that's precisely why she must leave him. James must be allowed to marry Jenny without all these entanglements. Still Charlotte's heart rebels, and doubt nags her even now.

The next morning, Charlotte again begs off when it's time to leave for mass. But this time, Luci furrows her brow.

"We have more than enough money to care for you and the baby when she comes. You needn't slip to the bank for more. You know that. Right?"

"Yes," Charlotte replies evasively.

Luci regards her skeptically, then shakes her head and leads her girls out the door.

Alone in the quiet house, Charlotte feels a stab of guilt. Slipping away with no explanation, merely a single note of gratitude and some coins, is an insult after all Nico and Luci have done for her. But she suspects they have more interest in keeping her content on St. Martin than helping her flee. Their marriage, after all, is a true love affair. They couldn't possibly understand. So, after collecting her things, she leaves a note in the kitchen, takes a final look around the charming home, and walks out the door.

At the bank, Charlotte secures delivery of her privateering gold to the ship, then tucks one key in her makeshift satchel and the other down her bodice. All that revenge, all that *thieving*, can finally serve her now. But when she arrives with a grateful smile to the *Sirène's* captain's cabin, Rainier is dour.

"I'm afraid we cannot leave today, madam," he says in French.

"Pardon me?" she asks, continuing in French.

"We await a final shipment, and it's been delayed."

"Delayed? You can't be delayed. We must leave today."

The captain shakes his head. "I'm sorry, madam." He glances at the large trunk delivered by the bank. "If you absolutely must leave today, perhaps there is another ship that can—"

"No, no. There's no *other* ship. It must be the *Sirène*, and it must be today."

"I can see you're distressed." Rainier glances at Charlotte's belly, then leads her to a chair. The man finds women and the workings of their bodies particularly unnerving. He believes himself gallant above all else, and the large trunk from the bank is intriguing, but he can't say he would be disappointed if the pregnant woman before him secured passage somewhere else.

"Please, sir. I cannot return to where I was staying."

"Your cabin is ready, madam. It is small and hardly intended for a woman, but it should suffice. If necessary, you may spend the night onboard."

Charlotte nods, thinking. "And what if he were to arrive here at the port and begin searching through the ships?"

"I can see you housed at the inn where I am staying." Once again the captain glances at the trunk. "Perhaps, for a small fee, we can secure a sailor to stand guard before your room. What does this man look like? What is his name?"

Charlotte's immediate fear is not James but Nico and Luci.

"He is tall and lean, has black hair and warm, olive skin."

A sailor whispers into Captain Rainier's ear, and the captain purses his lips and narrows his gaze. "This man, is he… Spanish?"

"No, sir." Charlotte's mind turns. "A Corsican."

"A Corsican. And you know this man…?"

Again the captain looks at Charlotte's belly, and she covers it.

"I'd rather not say."

The captain nods. At length, they peruse each other, then he says, "I'd like to help you, madam. Only tell me where you'd like to stay tonight, and we can secure you some protection."

"And some discretion?"

"But of course."

Charlotte appraises her cabin. Like her cabin aboard the *Anne*, this one is small, the ceiling hovering too close, with merely a narrow bed tucked into a corner. With the door closed, it makes her feel claustrophobic, and she has never been one to be anxious in tight spaces. After settling and securing her things, she is climbing the stairs to the main deck when she hears Nico's voice coming from the docks. He mentions the French flag and requests to speak with the captain, and Charlotte curses. Of course, the very thing that drew her drew him.

"I'm afraid the captain isn't aboard right now," the sailor explains.

"Where is he?"

"In the village. I couldn't say for certain. Probably enjoying one final stroll on land before we depart."

"You have a woman on board," Nico says. "I need to see her."

"There be no woman on board this ship."

"No?"

"No, sir."

"I think there is. She has red hair, she's fair, and she's pregnant. A conspicuous woman if ever there was one. You'll take me to her."

"I don't know about any woman on this here ship," the sailor says, his voice quavering now. Charlotte can only imagine what weapon Nico has brandished to turn the sailor's voice so tremulous. "Perhaps you'll go in search of the captain," he adds.

"Son, you seem like a fine enough fellow. I have no wish to hurt you, but I must see this woman. I intend her no harm. I mean only to speak with her."

"Seems to me every dangerous man says, 'I mean no harm.'"

"Stand aside," Nico persists.

"I can't do that, sir. I've a duty to the *Sirène* and to my captain."

"Stand aside, or you'll go for a swim," Nico says. "You *can* swim, can't you?"

There are sounds of boots scuffing on the deck, and another sailor calls out, "Rémy can swim, but you don't mean to suggest you'll board this ship without permission, do you, sir?"

"Would you be so kind as to grant me permission?"

"No."

There's the sound of carriage wheels clattering to a stop and a door swinging open. "What is the meaning of all this?" Captain Rainier says. "I must be disturbed from my noon meal to attend some foolish standoff at my ship? State your business, sir. Then be on your way."

"I would be happy to. May we speak in the privacy of your cabin?"

For Charlotte, there's an excruciating pause, then the captain says, "Of course, we may speak. Let's go to the inn where I'm eating."

"I'd rather not leave the docks," Nico says. "I'm particularly tetchy about losing things, and I suspect if I got into that carriage with you, I would lose something very dear to me. May I suggest again your cabin?"

Now there's a long pause, and Charlotte's heart is in her throat when the captain replies, "Very well, but I'm most unagreeable when I haven't eaten."

"As am I," Nico agrees.

While boots scrape across the gangplank, Charlotte races back to her cabin and closes the door, locks it and pushes her heavy trunk in front of it.

As for Nico, who's striding behind the captain, he's scanning every inch of the ship as they pass, imagining where Charlotte's hidden herself and feeling equal parts frustration and pride.

In the cabin, the captain, who is flanked by sailors, indicates a chair for Nico to sit in, and he does.

"What is all this?" Captain Rainier asks, his tone one of boredom.

"You have a woman in your safekeeping. I need to see her."

The captain exchanges a look of confusion with his sailors that is so patently feigned that Nico sighs.

"We have no woman in our safekeeping."

The sailors shake their heads.

"See here," Nico says, "if I was in any way uncertain before—and let's be clear, I wasn't—I have no doubt now. Where is she?"

"Of this you're so certain," Rainier says.

"You're bound for France. *She* is bound for France. And you don't seem to appreciate who I am. Your ignorance makes you foolish, but I like giving lessons."

The captain laughs uproariously, and his sailors follow suit. For a long moment, they delight in their amusement, until Rainer says, "Sir, are you honestly threatening me? One man against seven? It hardly seems fair."

Now it's Nico's turn to laugh, and as much as the captain and sailors delighted in their amusement, he delights in his own—until he reaches for his blade. It's then that the cabin door opens, and Charlotte stands framed in it.

"Baptiste, take your hand from that blade," she says, then to the sailors, "All of you, take your hands off your weapons."

Nico regards Charlotte with a wide smile. "My dear. I knew you were here."

"So you did."

Then the sailors move from the captain to flank Charlotte.

"What is this?" Nico asks. "Are you protecting her from me or me from her?"

Captain Rainer stands and adjusts his own blade in its sheath. "The lady claims she's being hunted by a murderous madman."

Nico chuckles. "Does she? Murderous, definitely. Mad, perhaps. You'll have to ask my wife. Some days, yes. Some days, no." Then he removes his blade so smoothly and quietly that it almost seems to be an illusion that his blade arm is not, in fact, twice the normal length, the tip hovering dangerously close to a sailor's ear. "But this gentlelady standing before you could best all of you, pregnant or no. Perhaps she could even best me."

Charlotte shakes her head, and Nico raises a brow.

"I promise you," Nico continues, "this woman is likely to be in greater danger from you than she is from me."

The captain regards Charlotte.

"Would you mind giving me a moment alone with him?" she asks.

Rainier looks at Nico's blade still poised near his sailor's neck.

"Please," she says.

Nico lowers his blade.

The captain sighs. "We'll be just outside this door, madam."

When the door latches behind them, Nico takes Charlotte in his arms and examines her. "Are you all right? What's happened? Why, all of a sudden, are you leaving now?"

Charlotte shrugs out of Nico's embrace. This, she knows, is how he works—penetrating kindness.

"It's time."

"So, just like that, you're leaving us."

Charlotte can't explain the strong pull she felt toward James the other night. How she felt her resolve to leave him vanishing. How, even now, his marrying Jenny seems a small obstacle compared to the love she feels for him, which is suddenly surging, not abating.

"I can't explain how I know. It's only that I feel him getting closer…"

"And there's nothing I can say to convince you?"

"My mind is made up."

Nico steps back and appraises Charlotte. With a soft smile he says, "I can see that you're determined, and I know very well a determined woman is a dangerous thing. Woe betide anyone who can't see that. I only ask you grant me one parting gift before you go."

Charlottes smiles indulgently. "Of course."

"You'll excuse this poor teacher's concern. I have done my very best with my best fencing student, but I can't quiet my fears. Even if you and the babe should survive this crossing, France is not safe. Bonaparte is amassing power, and royalists are still plotting their return."

"Is it so different than anywhere else I may go?"

The man sighs. "Perhaps not. You make too much damnable sense, woman. Promise me you'll never change."

"I promise."

"And I promise you, if James Blair should ever come for you, if I should determine he is an honorable man, I shall tell him all I know."

"I know you will. So, it's a good thing I have told you so little."

Nico and Charlotte embrace, and when they pull apart, he says, "Be wary. Be shrewd. Hold tight to your money. And don't hesitate to pull your blade. You're still dangerous, my dear. Make sure everyone around you knows it."

On the main deck, Captain Rainier watches while Charlotte waves goodbye to Nico. Then he beckons her to his cabin.

Seated at his desk, he appraises Charlotte skeptically and says, "Madam, I consider myself a chivalrous man when it comes to the care and keeping of women, but I'm finding I have some reservations as it regards helping you." Charlotte opens her mouth to speak, but he says,

"Because you lied to me. Did you not?"

"Captain, I… The man who just left here *is* murderous and has been trying to keep me here for some weeks, but only out of concern for my condition. I shaded some particulars, it's true, but I must sail to France with you, sir."

"Are you… still fleeing someone?"

"Yes, sir."

"But not this Baptiste."

"No."

"You're certain."

"Yes."

"That's good. That's very good. Because the infamous Baptiste is legendary for his singular appetite for mayhem when he is crossed."

"He wants only to see me safe."

"Then perhaps we could arrange some… payment. Now that I see you have the means."

"I'm most happy to pay a reasonable fee."

The captain glances at his dining table. "And, of course, I insist you join me for meals."

Charlotte looks at the table. "Of course."

The next afternoon, Charlotte stands on the dock saying goodbye to Nico and Luci and the girls, who've come to send her off.

"I think you foolish for leaving us when we could easily protect you here," Luci says, "but since you insist, you must go here and show them this." She thrusts a note into Charlotte's hand. "They will take you in."

Eventually, a sailor calls Charlotte aboard, and the *Sirène* weighs anchor and begins to drift away from the Marigot docks. On the main deck, Charlotte waves goodbye with a brave smile to the Bautistas. Still, inside, her heart is galloping in her chest. Once again she's setting off on a ship of strangers for the complete unknown.

5

Seven Stars, St. Croix

Weeks pass, and with each one, James grows more comfortable within his own mind and life. Now, in late August, he's been back home for nearly two months. And while some years of his life remain stubbornly locked away in his head, he's lost most of his desire to retrieve them.

Now James sits at his desk and breaks the seal of a T engraved in wax:

Dear Sir,

There are no words to adequately express the sincere joy I felt in reading your letter. At long last and well after I'd given up all hope, my niece, my dearly departed sister's daughter, is found.

I must humbly ask that you consider releasing Charlotte Dillon into my care...

The letter from the Countess of Tyrconnell goes on to tell of the home and family that await Charlotte and how the woman would forever be in his debt, but James can only peer dumbly at it. After Jenny's promise, he had expected to hear from the Crown, not some long-lost aunt of Charlotte's he has no recollection of writing.

At length, James stares at the lady's letter. He can feel her relief in her words. He knows he must write to her, but he has no idea what to say. Eventually, he realizes there's no help for it and pens a note to Keogh.

The next afternoon, James is sitting in his office when Keogh strides in. "You remember now?"

James indicates the chair before him and pours his friend a drink. When Keogh sits, James hands him the letter from Lady Tyrconnell.

"Mm-hmm," Keogh says while he reads.

The big man tells him what little he knows of the countess, that James sent for her to collect her niece.

"And now?" James asks.

"Now you have no choice but to tell the lady the truth."

"And that is?"

"You impregnated her niece and she fled. For St. Martin or perhaps points beyond."

"I can't write that. It's disgraceful."

Keogh nods.

"You needn't agree so easily," James says.

Keogh sets his glass down and wanders over to the bookshelves. "Do you know, you had a file once." He scrutinizes the spines. "A thick file from the Crown. All about Charlotte. Well, mostly about her crime, but… it was quite full of information. If only you could find that, perhaps it would trigger your memory."

Now James wanders over to the shelves and peers at them. In truth, he's barely looked at them since he's been back, so engrossed has he been in getting his affairs in order. "I kept it?"

"I don't know. I only know how you were that day when you read it."

James looks at Keogh, urging.

"When you thought her dead, you… We all grieved, but you… You wrote to the Crown for more information. Six months after you thought her dead, you tortured yourself reading that file. You just wanted to know her, you said."

"And did I?" James asks, looking back again at the shelves. "Come to know her?"

Keogh shrugs.

A short time later, he leaves, and James, still having no idea what he will write to the countess, strolls back to the shelves. There he drags his fingers down spine after spine—books on sailing and sugar planting, import and export logs from his shipping office, logs from his lost years on the workings of Seven Stars. It's a veritable treasure trove of his lost life, and as the sun arcs through the sky and light in the office dims, he lights his desk lamp and leans into his papers, devouring them all. He reads on and on, year by year—the strains of sugarcane he imported, the yields he's increased, the shipping fleet he grew.

Over the days that follow, James reads all of it, until finally he comes to a thick file with no spine hidden between some books of fiction. Pulling it out, he spies the seal of the Chief Secretary of Ireland, and his heart begins to race. He sits, and with great anticipation pulls the red ribbon. Inside, he finds a letter:

Dear Sir,

I thank you for informing me of the fate of your convict, No. JR-914.

However, there seems to be some confusion, for the last name and manner of death you provided for this convict do not match her files here.

Convict No. JR-914 belongs to a Miss Charlotte Dillon...

James's breath leaves him. This is the very file he was searching for. Eagerly, he reads on, following Charlotte through her life, her name, her birthplace, her parents, the workhouse run by the Franciscan sisters, her employment as a maid for the Lord Chancellor and his family at Mountshannon, and her crime—the heir to the Crown's most powerful man in Ireland stabbed through the heart with a cobbler's awl.

The daughter of republican agitator Charles Dillon. A tory rebel, some say. An assassin. Then James spies her defense—self-defense, that the Lord Chancellor's sons were trying to rape her. And near the bottom of the file, a letter from the Countess of Tyrconnell to the Chief Secretary of Ireland pleading for information on her niece.

Finally, James exhales and stares at the sea of papers spread across his desk. Now, it seems, he knows everything, and still he remembers nothing. Perhaps more importantly, James *feels* nothing. Never could he have imagined how much hope lay in reading this file. Now that he has and it yielded none of what everyone presumed it would, James believes that empty feeling is as sure a sign as anything. There's only one more thing he must do.

He puts quill to parchment:

> Dear Lady Tyrconnell,
>
> In shame, I write to inform you that your niece, The Hon. Charlotte Dillon, has gone missing.
>
> I regret now that I didn't share with her my plans for you to collect her, for it appears she believed herself in an untenable position here. Desperate, she escaped without a word to anyone.
>
> Though I have searched, there remains pure conjecture. She is fluent in French and may reside on Saint-Domingue or Saint Martin, though the leads I've followed have born no fruit.
>
> I'm afraid I cannot devote more of my time to searching the Caribbean, or indeed the world, for an indenture I had planned to free of her contract.
>
> As to that, consider this my official notice that convict No. JR-914 The Hon. Charlotte Dillon, is now free of the bonds of her indenture. Given these most unusual circumstances, of course, you owe me nothing.
>
> In humble service,
> The Hon. James Blair

It is easily the most dishonorable letter James has ever written.

Somewhere in the Atlantic Ocean

Three weeks later, Charlotte walks the deck of the *Sirène*, breathing in salt and brine. Twice each day she is allowed this exercise on the main deck, and she delights greedily in every moment.

Then footsteps approach, the crisp and confident stride she's grown to know well of Captain Rainier.

"Captain," she says.

"Madam." He sighs. "I'm afraid we have some weather approaching. It may, in fact, be a trifle more than passing rain this time."

Charlotte peers into the distance to see steel-gray clouds rolling in.

"When the rains come, I ask that you retreat to your cabin and hold tight…" He regards her belly. "For your safety."

Hours later, wind and rain lash the ship, and it pitches and sways violently. In her cabin, Charlotte sits, bracing herself against the wall at her back and pressing her feet to the bed. Less than an hour has she done this, and her rangy muscles are quivering with fatigue. Determining that all the clenching can't be good for the baby, Charlotte examines the bedstead, then her gaze flits around the small cabin until it falls on the rope handles of her trunk, and an idea forms.

Crawling to the door, Charlotte opens it and, desperately clutching the walls, makes her way out to the hold.

"Madam," a sailor cries, "what are you about? Return to your cabin at once. It isn't safe."

The sailor, a man who is younger and weaker than Charlotte, grabs hold of her and tries to drag her back.

"No, sir!" she cries, locking her legs. "I need rope. Sturdy rope to fashion into handles."

The young man stops and looks around. "Yes, madam. Of course. Let's get you back to your cabin, and I'll bring it."

Once Charlotte is settled again, the sailor leaves and shortly returns with the rope. She fashions a handle at the bedstead, and the sailor, spying her industry, begins doing the same. Moments later, there are four hanks of rope tied to the bed.

Charlotte climbs onto the feather mattress and looks to the sailor. "Tie my ankles."

"Madam?"

"Tie them. If I must brace myself through this entire storm, I will lose my babe, and I'll blame you."

The sailor gulps and ties her ankles with the rough rope.

"Tighter, sailor. Please."

"But, madam, if the hold fills with water..."

"If this hold fills with water, I'll drown regardless of what we do. Now do it."

The sailor binds her ankles to the bed, then he looks at Charlotte and gulps. She lies back with a smile of thanks and grasps the rope handles she fastened. "You'll come to check on me once the storm has passed?"

"Yes, madam. Whenever I can."

When the sailor leaves, Charlotte holds fast to the ropes while the wind howls, the rain pelts, and the ship climbs and careens. All the while, her stomach reaches into her throat and dips into her gut. Clumsily, she begins to pray.

In this way, an endless age seems to pass. From time to time, the young sailor dutifully checks on her. Until, finally, the raging storm begins to calm, and as the ship settles her bows to the waves once more, Charlotte, her nerves and muscles strained, slips gratefully to sleep.

6

Faire Abbey, Paris, France

The ship weathered the storm with little damage and, weeks later, made landfall in La Rochelle. After another week traveling over land to Paris, now in early October, Charlotte stands before a grand building under a majestic dome while carriages bearing Parisians go by behind her. Clutching the note Luci gave her when they parted, she looks down at the name written on it, then peers at the matching name forged into an iron plaque above the inscription:

"Whither you are bound, take rest."

Ever since the hills of St. Martin faded into the distance, Charlotte has been cursing herself for a fool. Who crosses an ocean, a difficult enough journey without being pregnant, while six months with child? Now here she is, at the Cistercian abbey Luci promised would take her in, and a broken sob escapes her lips when she clutches her belly.

Then the tall doors swing open, and a woman in a black habit, a white wimple, and a gold pectoral cross stands before her.

"Oh, Mother Abbess," Charlotte says in French, "I'm so grateful to be here at last."

The abbess spies the trunk and Charlotte's things, then Charlotte hands her Luci's note. The abbess reads it, then scrutinizes her.

"We can house you, Madam…?" the abbess lifts an urging brow.

On the long journey, Charlotte has given this some thought. She knows she must choose a French surname to aid in her story, but her mind still drifts to that magical summer day on the hilltop at Seven Stars when James first asked her to marry him. If she can't be Mistress Blair, she can still be reminded of that hilltop, so she chooses a French name that means "lovely hill."

"Madam Beaumont," Charlotte replies.

"We require perfect silence except in prayer."

Charlotte nods earnestly.

"Follow me."

Just beyond the main gatehouse, they walk through a garden while browning leaves crunch under their feet. In Paris in October, the air in shade is laced with the winter to come, and Charlotte clutches her wrap tightly.

Inside, the abbey is spare stacked stone, walls and arches and underfoot, an enduring sturdiness to match the steadfast devotion practiced within it. They pass rows of solemn young ladies, daughters of diplomats and God-fearing girls, all dressed in severe gray gowns and bound in silence, their daring eyes flitting up at the newcomer before going by. A current of balsam oil heralds a candlelit chapel, graced with garnet glass and limned in incense with heads bent in prayer.

Then they go up and up wide flagstone stairs, Charlotte's driver grunting loudly with each step under the weight of her trunk. The abbess is a lioness to her pride of ladies and only concedes a man this far into the depths of the abbey to perform this burdensome task. Still, the man annoys her, and halfway up the stairs, she stops and regards him with imperious exasperation. So, he claps his mouth shut and adjusts his load.

At the top of the stairs, they carry on through a transomed hallway, past a drawing room with silk-tufted settees, Queen Anne chairs and tables, and a warm fire in the fireplace. Three women dressed in elegant daywear, one holding a little girl of three or four, sit sewing and chatting, and when Charlotte passes, they stop talking to regard her.

Then the abbess leads Charlotte and her driver down another long hallway to a door and unlocks it to reveal a quaint suite of rooms.

"Your apartment, madam," the abbess utters.

When Charlotte turns to thank the abbess, the woman is already striding out the door. The driver heaves his load onto the floor with a grateful sigh, then looks at Charlotte expectantly. She hands him some coins, and the man turns on a heel and leaves.

Flopping onto her bed, tears well in Charlotte's eyes while she tenderly rubs her belly. "Now you can come, baby girl."

Charlotte sleeps the sleep of the dead and wakes to find squares of late-morning light streaming through the mullion of her arch windows. Sore from lying sprawled out like a drunk across her bed, Charlotte groans when she stands. Her stomach rumbles, then she hears voices coming from down the hall.

Opening her door, a distinctive sweet and tangy aroma wafts Charlotte's way, and she wanders down to the drawing room.

There, the ladies and the girl stop chatting to regard her. Before them on a table sits a basket filled with tropical fruits. Charlotte's mouth waters, and she swallows, then looks to the women. Her mouth falls open to speak, but chastened by the abbess, she pauses. Eventually, she whispers, "Are those what I think they are?"

"Depends," one woman replies. "What do you think they are?"

"I think they're oranges, pineapples, and mangoes," Charlotte replies.

"However did you guess that?" another woman asks. "I'd never heard of them until the lady dropped off her basket last month, and I was new here then."

"None of us had ever tried them until Madam de La Rose's delivery," the third woman replies, peeling an orange for the little girl.

After they introduce themselves, Madam de La Court asks, "Are you from the West Indies, then?"

"Might I ask," Charlotte says, "how is it you're speaking so freely when the abbess warned me to silence. The girls I saw yesterday…"

Madam de La Court regards Madam Simon and they share a laugh. But Madam Fortin, whose hair has skeins of gray in it, side-eyes the younger women, then looks kindly to Charlotte, and says, "Sins of the tongue. They don't want their young charges to succumb to idle talk as girls are wont to do. But they must look the other way for us."

"They need our money, of course," Madam Simon says, feeding a wedge of orange to her daughter, Lilou, who gnaws hungrily on it, letting the juice slip down her chin.

"Yours, too, I suspect," Madam de La Court adds, "or you wouldn't be here."

"Come, sit with us, my dear," Madam Fortin says, "before your time is come right here on the rug. You must tell us how you know this fruit, and we'll gladly share some."

Straffan Hall, County Kildare, Ireland
When the Countess of Tyrconnell spies James Blair's seal in the midst of her letters, her heart soars. Hastily, she cracks it open and reads, then loses her breath and falls back in her chair.

"My lady," her maid, Quinn, says, "is something the matter?"

Adelle looks at Quinn, her mouth agape and her face a picture of torment.

"What is it?" the maid continues. "Shall I get you some tea? Perhaps you should lie down. I'll call the earl—"

"No," the lady says. "No." She shakes her head. "I mean I needn't lie down, but, yes, call the earl. I need to speak to him."

Moments later, the Earl of Tyrconnell strides into his wife's dressing room. "Is something amiss?"

Adelle hands her husband James's letter.

"Blair," Stephen utters, his voice laced with frustration. "He is ever…" But his voice trails off as he reads, then he looks up. "She's missing? What kind of a man can he be if she thought herself so desperate as to flee him? He must be a scourge."

Adelle shakes her head. "I can't credit it. His previous letters… All of them showed a man with honor and compassion, a man effusive in his praise of her. In truth, I think, a man who had a tenderness for her. But this…" Again the lady shakes her head.

"This paints a very different picture," the lord says.

Tightlipped and jaw locked, Adelle bites out, "I'm so frustrated I could scream." The lady's cheeks color with her cresting fury. "She is fluent in French and could reside on Saint-Domingue or St. Martin. But if she has a facility with language, she could be anywhere, Stephen!"

The earl nods.

"How could he let her go?" the lady continues.

"It doesn't appear that it was a matter of letting her…"

Adelle glares at her husband.

"He went in search of her," Stephen continues. "I don't know that I can fault the man for not finding her or not continuing."

"*I* can. She is his responsibility."

Absently, the earl nods while he regards the letter again. "It seems he's washed his hands of her."

"He's a disgrace to leave her to the Fates," the countess says.

"Is there something of your own guilt nagging you?" the earl asks.

"No."

Stephen gives her a scolding brow.

"There isn't," she insists. "She is his responsibility."

"My dear, she is no child, and I suspect, if she is anything like her aunt, that she is a clever and determined woman."

Fuming, Adelle turns away from her husband and begins to pace while she conceives a plan. "I have no choice. I shall have to pay him to find his own lost indenture."

"A moment ago you called Blair a disgrace. Now you would enlist him to search for Charlotte?"

The lady shrugs.

"He's no mercenary that you can pay," the lord says. "He's a planter."

"Every planter that I know can use the money, and disgrace or no, Blair is the only link to Charlotte that I have."

Port of Dublin, Dublin

Days later, the Countess of Clare turns against the rank gusts that blow off the Liffey. Yet more than the wind, the lady can't escape the certainty she feels that this trip will bring more heartbreak and not less.

"You should arrive by Christmas," the earl says, shaking Lord Peter's hand.

"Write of your safe arrival as soon as you can," the countess says.

"I'll do that, my lady."

On the gangplank, the young lord turns back. Still hopeful her son might change his mind, Lady Clare straightens and beams, but Lord Peter merely waves a final time.

"Give my warmest greetings to Joanna for me, please," Lady Clare says.

"I will."

Faire Abbey, Paris, France

On the morning of twenty-fourth October, Charlotte wakes with a heavy feeling in her stomach, not quite pain and not quite nausea. She's been battling peculiar twinges for some weeks, weighing her fears and ignorance each time a new pain surges and passes, but this is unlike anything she's ever felt.

Climbing out of bed, Charlotte shrugs into a robe and shuffles to the drawing room. "Madams," she calls, her voice high-pitched and small. But it's early yet—the fire isn't lit, and no one is about.

Charlotte looks up at the soaring dome above. Light steals in through the mosaic of colors in the stained-glass plate tracery. It's meant to be awe-inspiring, yet pain squeezes her gut and terror licks down her spine. Never has she wanted her mother so much as now, when the only companion she has is the majestic silence.

Charlotte huffs in despair, goes to Madam Fortin's door, and knocks. "Madam," she calls. "I'm so sorry to wake you, but… I think my time has come."

"One moment, madam." There are hurried sounds, shuffling of bed clothes and clothing being donned. Then, after some long moments, footsteps approach, and the door opens to reveal Madam Fortin. "This pain you feel is... different? A first-time mother can be plagued by more than pain."

"I think it is different," Charlotte says. She wonders for a moment, then adds, "It is."

Madam Fortin nods. "Then you must dress and pack a small bag. Can you manage that?"

Charlotte nods.

"I'll ring for a carriage."

"A carriage? I can't travel like this."

"Not far. To the Hôtel-Dieu. It is the best lying-in hospital in Paris. You must be delivered there. It is the only place I would send my own daughter. Now go and ready yourself."

The plan dulls the sharp edge of Charlotte's fear, and she returns to her apartment, dresses, and packs. In the hallway, she is greeted by the well-wishes of Madams de La Court and Simon, then she laces her arm through Madam Fortin's, and together they descend to meet the carriage.

The ride to the Hôtel-Dieu is less than thirty minutes, but the jostling and the frequent stops on the busy Paris streets while enduring the persistent squeezing pain around her middle... To Charlotte, it feels like the longest ride of her life. Eventually, the carriage stops before an ecru stone building as long as a city block.

Within, Madam Fortin gives Charlotte a kiss for luck and hands her over to a young Breton woman named Violette who is training in midwifery. Then she's brought to a massive room with soaring arches that reach skyward several stories. Shafts of light pierce plate-stained glass, and wrought-iron lanterns dangle down, shedding musky-smelling whale oil and light through cranberry glass.

Struck by the beauty, it's only when they've walked half the length of the nave-like room that Charlotte lowers her gaze. Along the walls lie bed after bed, nearly every one of them full. Many of the women, in the throes of labor, have faces and bodies contorted in pain. Some moan. Some cry out. Some lie listless. Some lie sated with babes in arms. But nearly all of them wear the hard-bitten face of the poor.

When Violette stops before an empty bed, one of a handful set apart by embroidered screens, Charlotte says, "I'm to be delivered here?" Just then, water trickles down her legs, puddling onto the flagstone.

The young nurse smiles and says, "Let's get you out of your dress, madam, and into a nice warm bath."

Violette, practiced in service and composed in crisis, sets to helping Charlotte out of her dress. Meanwhile, a large copper tub is filled with steaming lavender water, and soon enough she is helped into it. Eventually, the screen is wrapped around Charlotte's birthing suite, and the nurse departs, promising to be back shortly. While the water's heat steals into her muscles, Charlotte spies a painting of a woman kneeling, her hands clasped in prayer and her beseeching gaze fixed up at a heavenly light.

Nearby, a woman wails, then Charlotte's belly seizes up, and she lurches forward with a small sob. *I'm going to die here*, she thinks, wretchedly. She tries to peer around the screen, to track the imperious *clacking* of her nurses boots on the flagstone. But in this church filled with women, Charlotte seems to be entirely alone.

Hours drag on, during which Charlotte's labor pains steadily increase. After being helped out of the tub, she paces, breathing and bracing and praying. From time to time, she's examined, and her labor is pronounced as progressing well.

When the sun has long since gone down and shadows reach into the room, more lamps are lit along with candles and candelabras. The once-cold space grows warm, and smoke mingles with the metallic smell of blood. Then Charlotte is examined, and for the first time the nurse does not smile.

"What is it?" Charlotte asks with her heart in her throat.

Violette helps her back into bed and stalks off. Returning moments later, she helps Charlotte sit up, then hands her a cup. "Drink it all."

"What is this? What is happening?"

"Nothing whatever for you to worry about, madam. It's only that your labor has slowed. If you drink this syrup of ipecac, it should produce the convulsions we need."

Charlotte peers into the cup. "Convulsions?"

"In your belly, madam. It's perfectly natural. I assure you. Now drink it down, please."

Yet Charlotte knows of ipecac. Beyond the excruciating pain she feels, it will certainly make her violently ill. She gives Violette a pleading look, but the nurse only nods, her jaw set. Charlotte swallows the sugary-tasting syrup in one gulp, then lies back and waits.

Soon enough, her stomach begins to bend. Charlotte vomits over and over until all that remains is bile and dry heaving. Periodically, she is examined, and still Violette shakes her head. The pressure and the pain are beyond anything Charlotte could have ever conceived, and now her stomach has been revolting with no change. A broken sob escapes Charlotte, and tears stream down her cheeks.

Again Violette stalks off, this time returning with a leather strap, a lancet, and a bowl. Exposing Charlotte's arm, the nurse binds it with the leather and traces her finger along the crook of Charlotte's elbow to find a vein. Charlotte, nauseous still, in agony, and depleted, drags her listless eyes to her elbow and moans as Violette pierces her skin with the lancet.

"Your humors are almost certainly blocked, madam, preventing the labor from progressing," the nurse explains while a trickle of blood flows into a bowl. "We need to breathe the vein."

Charlotte can only nod.

More time goes by. It's late at night now, and the pain pressing down on Charlotte's low back is pure torture. She would reposition herself in bed to alleviate it if only she had the strength. But she feels as weak as the cold rag being dragged across her forehead. Her stamina is fading, her mind is fading, and all she can do is call out for James.

"Jamie!"

Never has Charlotte wanted to be with James more than now, in what she is certain are the last moments of her and her daughter's life. Charlotte would live to see her child take her first breaths, but in the blurry space between agony and defeat, she would do anything, even welcome death, for her torment to end.

Then, through bleary eyes, Charlotte sees a new woman standing by her bed. Madam Lachapelle wears a tight, brown gown and a ruffled cream collar. She appraises Charlotte with astute eyes, then glances disdainfully at Violette. Throwing her covers back, the head of obstetrics muscles a limp Charlotte up, barking at the nurse, "Help me get her into the birthing chair right now!"

"Madam?" Violette says, scrambling to lift Charlotte's other side.

Working together, the two women heft their bundle onto a seatless chair, and there, Madam Lachapelle peels her sleeves back and examines Charlotte while she whimpers and moans.

Madam Lachapelle glowers at Violette. "You've been purging and bleeding her for hours now?"

Violette nods.

"Then you've depleted the very thing this woman and her baby need to survive."

"Madam?"

"Go to the kitchens. Get pitchers of water and almond milk, skins of honey, and some liver pâté and bring them back immediately. This woman needs to be revived so she can be delivered of her babe. Now go!"

"You mean to feed her, madam?"

Madam Lachapelle glares at Violette, who skitters away.

Then the head midwife looks at Charlotte, whose eyes droop. Madam Lachapelle reaches inside her and turns the baby, which has precisely the effect the woman desired. The pain that rips through Charlotte's belly makes her suck in a breath and open her eyes, arch her back and holler.

"Good," Madam Lachapelle says. "You're back with us. And just in time, for I've moved your baby into a better position to come."

Charlotte regards the hardheaded woman and thinks either the head midwife has gone mad or she has. "Leave me to die, only do something for the pain."

"I shall do," Madam Lachapelle says. "The best thing for the pain is to get the baby out. If you mean to die, you've come to the wrong hospital. Now bear down and push."

For nearly an hour, Charlotte pushes, choking down food and liquids all throughout. Until, eventually, as morning dawns, she is delivered.

"A fine boy," Madam Lachapelle declares while she scrubs and bundles him.

Finally, when mother and baby are clean and curled up together, Charlotte looks down at her son's—*a son!*—deep-water blue eyes peering cannily up at her and says, "Jamie."

Seven Stars, St. Croix

James wakes suddenly, feeling a deep and tender pull in his heart.

7

A week later, James spies a letter from the Crown, sits, and cracks the seal:

Dear Sir,

I have recently received a most curious letter. It tells of your capture of the wanted pirate Back from the Dead Red...

James reads as it recounts serious allegations against Charlotte and an unlikely web of conspiracy. Clearly, Miss Lund managed to do exactly what she claimed, and now he must decide whether or how much he cares.

Governor-General's Residence, Christiansted

The very next afternoon, James is admitted into Governor-General Lund's office. There he sits before the governor-general, who regards him with icy politeness.

"I thank you for admitting me," James says.

"I'm not in the habit of slighting people, Mr. Blair, regardless of what occurred between you and my daughter. I'm keen to see us come to some accord."

"As am I. That's why I felt it important that I share this with you."

James withdraws the Crown letter and hands it to Governor-General Lund, who dons his spectacles and reads it, his brow narrowing, his mouth falling open, and his cheeks turning a livid red.

Eventually, he slams the letter down and strides to the door, flings it open, and bellows, "*JENNY! GET DOWN HERE THIS VERY INSTANT!*"

"You'll pardon me, sir," James says, "I thought it best we discuss this without your daughter."

In truth, there's been a part of James that has been curious about Miss Lund ever since that day in the garden. In his sieve-like mind, he was meeting Jenny for the first time as a woman, and he felt an instant and rare attraction to her. Yet to hear Keogh describe their relationship, Jenny was single-minded in her pursuit of him, perhaps to the point of obsession, and certainly manipulative. James has filed this away in his mind—Jenny is this; Charlotte is that. Still, facts are one thing. Feelings are altogether another. James has no feelings for Charlotte, but Jenny…

She appears in the doorway in a petal-pink gown that enhances the color on her cheeks. "Yes, Father?"

James stands, and Jenny regards him with a glower, to which he responds with a soft smile. He can't help but like a beautiful woman who so completely despises him.

The governor-general glares down at his daughter. "Pray, tell me exactly what you think you've done with Mr. Blair."

Jenny looks quizzically at James, then back to the governor-general. "I don't know what you mean, Father."

"You don't know what I mean?" the man yells, brandishing the Crown letter.

Jenny takes the letter and reads it, then colors. Her mouth falls open while her mind turns. "I'm sorry, Father, but my seal on Mr. Blair's letter would have seen it dismissed."

"You would rather see your father embroiled in an international intrigue?"

"Of course not. How was I to know of this engagement at Copenhagen?"

"That is precisely my point, daughter. Women, with their fripperies, have no business in such affairs. You had no right to forge a man's name and send a letter that did not belong to you!" the governor-general says, his voice growing louder, until he's hollering at the end.

Then the door bursts open to reveal Joanna Lund waving her handkerchief at her bodice. Spying James, she scowls. "Of course, this has something to do with you, Mr. Blair."

"Madam, I am only the messenger," James says. "It is your daughter—"

"Our daughter," the governor-general says, "in her rejection, has sought to avenge her broken heart and has managed to place me, by the use of *my* seal, at the fulcrum of a potentially desperate international incident."

Mrs. Lund's face grows blanched, and her eyes flutter.

Jenny meets James's eyes and gives him a fleeting look of exasperation, then goes to her mother. "Sit, please, before you faint."

"How shall we remedy this?" Governor-General Lund asks.

"I thought we might each write a letter," James says, "explaining in our way that Miss Lund was mistaken."

"So, together you will conspire to belittle me," Jenny says, looking between James and her father.

"If it should get me out of the corner you've put me in," the governor-general says, "I shall be happy to make you this tall." He holds up his pinky and frames the tip of it.

Jenny reddens and pulls her lips into a rigid line.

"Would you rather I do something else?" James asks, his tone of voice not taunting but soft and solicitous.

Jenny glares at him. "Are you quite done here, Mr. Blair?"

"I don't know," he says, smiling stupidly.

Keogh's Residence

A short time later, James stands in Keogh's drawing room with an awestruck smile on his face. "Would it be so terrible if I have some…

feelings for Miss Lund?"

Keogh regards James as if he's gone mad. "Yes."

"Yes?"

"Have you forgotten what I told you? Obsessive. Manipulative."

"Couldn't one just as equally say devoted and clever?" James says.

"One could say that."

"But you'll not."

Keogh shakes his head.

"Why not?"

"Jamie, what has got into you?

James turns this over in his mind, then says, "She hates me so. I can't help but respect her for it."

Keogh rolls his eyes. "Do you know who hates you? Charlotte. Charlotte hates you. She hates you so much she fled with your babe inside. Now *that* is a pure commitment to hating you. Think on that."

"I can't think on that. I feel nothing for her still."

Keogh puts his heavy hands on James's shoulders. "Son, it's early November. Your babe has almost certainly been delivered by now. You have a child in this world that you've not seen. If you'll not think on his mother, then think on him."

Faire Abbey, Paris, France

A month later, Charlotte stands with six-week-old baby Jamie in her arms. Wind whistles through the mullion in her windows, and a cold rain pelts the leaded glass, but her apartment's warm brazier glows, and as she coos, the baby's blue eyes track the sound of her voice.

Two weeks Charlotte remained at the Hôtél Dieu for her lying-in, and each day confined to her bed was longer than the last. For many days after giving birth, she was weak and feverish. Tucked tightly into her bed, she lay mostly alone but for when the nurses brought the baby. Vital and strong from the first, the boy—whom she christened James Charles after his father and her father—took hungrily to her breast.

When Charlotte returned to the abbey, what followed was a four-week haze of holding and feeding, staring and sleeping, confusion and exhaustion. Never has she cared less about herself and more about another person, and never could she imagine what a gift that would be. Now when she thinks of the fears she held when she was pregnant, she blushes in shame. For never could she imagine loving someone more.

On this day, Charlotte wanders down to the drawing room and finds a new woman standing amongst the ladies. At the sound of Charlotte's footsteps, the woman turns and bestows a beatific smile on her.

"Ah! So, we finally meet."

Madam de La Rose has alabaster skin and chocolate-brown hair styled up with a few curls that frame a face just turning toward middle age. The woman sets down the basket she bore and holds out her hands, indicating the baby. "May I hold him?"

Reluctantly, Charlotte hands Jamie over to her, and they sit. Madam de La Rose expertly rocks her legs back and forth, examining the baby wistfully. All the while, Jamie sleeps.

"You have the touch, madam," Charlotte says.

Without looking up, Madam de La Rose says, "I have two of my own. Grown now. But I would give anything for another. If only for my husband." The fire pops and crackles. "What of your husband, Madam Beaumont?"

"Slain," Charlotte chokes out the lie.

"In the fighting on Saint-Domingue?"

"Yes."

"They told me as much. And how long were you in the West Indies?" When Charlotte doesn't immediately answer, the woman looks at her and says, "That is not a Creole accent, for I know it well."

"Nearly four years, by way of Ireland."

"That is how you know my offerings so well."

Charlotte looks longingly at the basket. "Yes, madam. The sight and smell... They remind me of my husband." Heat floods into her cheeks.

Madam de La Rose cocks her head, her brows knit with compassion. "It was a love match," she says.

"Yes."

Madam de La Rose hands the still-sleeping Jamie back to Charlotte, who cradles him all the tighter.

"Oh, my dear girl, you're so very alone now?"

Charlotte nods.

"Do you know, I lived here once," Madam de La Rose says. "I was at the mercy of an uncaring husband, and they took me in. That is a terrible prison, to be married to a heartless man."

"There are worse prisons," Charlotte says without thinking.

A sly smile curls the corners of Madam de La Rose's mouth. "Indeed, there are." The woman scrutinizes Charlotte for a long moment. "You must come and see my orangerie, Madam Beaumont."

"I couldn't impose."

"It's no imposition. We women of the West Indies should be bosom friends."

Madam de La Rose leaves shortly after that, and the women swarm around Charlotte to muse and tease.

"You will be her new favorite," Madam Simon declares.

"Her pet," Madam de La Court adds.

"Do you think I should go?" Charlotte asks Madam Fortin.

"Of course, you must," Madam Fortin says. "You cannot turn down such an invitation."

"No?" Charlotte asks.

"Madam de La Rose is not her actual name, silly," Madam de La Court says. "It's only that she prefers to slip in and out of Paris *incognitus*."

"You truly don't know who she is?" Madam Simon asks.

"Should I?"

"That is the wife of France's First Consul—Napoleon Bonaparte."

Seven Stars, St. Croix

On Christmas Eve, James is sifting through correspondence when he spies a letter from the Countess of Tyrconnell. The heat of shame floods into his cheeks while he stares at it for some moments. Eventually, his curiosity cresting, he cracks the seal and reads:

> *Dear Sir,*
>
> *There are no words to express the dismay I felt in reading your recent letter. Keen to learn how I might collect her, instead I am confronted with the news that my niece is now gone missing.*
>
> *I must prevail upon you, sir, to find her for me, whatever the cost. You are the only link I have to her. Toward that end, I have established a line of funds with your island bank. Take leave to use it however you might need, even to hire a mercenary who can find her for me.*
>
> *There is nothing I would not do to secure my niece's safety and happiness. So, I look forward to your swift reply with the news that your search, whether through yourself or a trusted agent, has resumed with all haste.*
>
> *In humble request,*
> *The Countess of Tyrconnell*

James regards the letter, considering all the countess requires. Given what Keogh said of the mail packet, the very least James owes the countess is a sincere inquiry on the island of St. Martin. Yet there's a part of him that can admit he fears what he might confront if he should ever find Charlotte—namely that, like Shea and others, he won't remember her. Still, he has an abiding curiosity about his child.

Governor-General's Residence

On Christmas Day, the Lunds dine with their new houseguest. Lord Peter Fitzgibbon had arrived from Ireland only two days before, desperate to confront James Blair. Still, for propriety's sake, he must bide his time over the holiday.

Governor-General Lund regards the young lord critically. Lord

Peter, with his lean body and baby face, appears unequal to confront any man. Lund squirms, feeling uneasy for some reason he can't quite understand. Wiping his mouth, he says, "You're here on a matter of some import as regards one of our planters?"

"Yes," Peter replies.

"Which planter, my lord?" Jenny asks.

Mrs. Lund directs a scolding brow at her daughter, then turns to their guest with a bland smile. "Of course, it certainly isn't any of our affair." Though Mrs. Lund is positively brimming with curiosity.

"I suppose I do owe you some candor," the young lord says, and the governor-general and Mrs. Lund sit forward. "I'm here to see Mr. Blair."

Joanna's face falls. "He is a reprobate, my lord. You would do well to steer clear of him."

"Mr. Blair was to be our son by now…" The governor-general glances at Jenny, who blushes and glares. "But he had a change of heart."

Peter regards Jenny, whom he's found particularly enchanting over the past two days. "I find it hard to credit how any man could set you aside, miss, when you're the very picture of loveliness."

Jenny blushes, for she does believe herself the picture of loveliness. "You're too kind, my lord. It's only that he strummed one of his indentures, and while some may look the other way at this, I shall play second fiddle to no woman."

"Strum," Joanna says, dabbing a handkerchief furiously at her décolletage. "Must we discuss such crude things? It is Christmas, after all."

The next day, Jenny sidles up to Lord Peter walking in the garden. Ever since dinner the night before, all through the night and this morning, she has been unable to quiet her mind about the young lord's business with Mr. Blair. "Won't you please tell me why it is you've come all the way to St. Croix to speak with Mr. Blair?"

Peter hesitates. He is, by nature, circumspect, and the woman before him, however enchanting, seems a keen gossip. Then he muses that the island and her inhabitants will see the back of him for good soon enough, and what does he care what they say of him?

"Mr. Blair indentured some convicts to work on his plantation."

"Yes."

"One of whom murdered my brother. She was supposed to hang. Instead, she came here to this beautiful island and lived for another year or more until, apparently, she was killed in a pirate attack."

"You must be mistaken. There haven't been any pirate attacks on the island in many years. There was a kidnapping, but she's not dead…" Illumination dawns. Jenny knows Peter can only be referring to one woman, and luckily for her, it's the woman she despises most in the world. "I know the woman you seek, my lord. In fact, she's now, almost certainly, the mother of Mr. Blair's child."

Lord Peter's mouth falls open. "Pardon me?"

"You say this woman killed your brother?"

"Where is she? At his plantation all this time? Even now?"

"No. Not anymore. In truth, I don't know."

"Don't be coy, miss. I beg you. I would give anything to see justice done for my brother."

"I'm not being coy, I promise you. She was at Seven Stars, then fled the island for… God only knows where.

"Mr. Blair knows."

"No. He went in search of her and returned without her. 'Twas not the woman, you see, but the child. He wants his son, I suppose."

"You mean to tell me this woman bore him a child and he has no idea where she is?"

"As far as I know, my lord, she's lost."

8

Château de Malmaison, France

Through the twelve days of Christmas, while the other ladies have left Faire Abbey to visit family, Charlotte accepts Madam Bonaparte's invitation to visit. After a dreary ride through Paris, the Seine opens up to a pastoral countryside, and eventually the carriage comes to a stop before a grand, three-story wheat-colored château.

In the foyer, Josephine greets Charlotte and Jamie warmly. "You've made it to my delicious spot. Let's get you settled. I'm mad for your opinion on my orangerie."

After Charlotte and Jamie are shown to a suite of rooms and the baby is handed over into the care of a nursemaid, Charlotte strolls arm-in-arm with Josephine out to a separate building. Stepping in, the cold and barren world outside is instantly replaced by the heady tang of sweet citrus and a humid warmth that assails her with memories.

Josephine leads Charlotte under a soaring glass dome, wending through row upon row of potted palms and citrus. Hundreds of varieties of fruits and flowers, including vivid white, yellow, and orange hibiscus flowers. At a pineapple plant, Charlotte inhales and smiles drunkenly.

"It's the fragrance," Josephine says. "There is nothing that calls to mind the cherished memories of the sugar plantation on which I was raised more than these intoxicating smells."

"You were raised on a sugar plantation, madam?"

The woman nods. "Have you some familiarity with sugar planting?"

"Some," Charlotte says.

Josephine beams. "Then it is settled. We are meant to be friends."

Days pass, much of them Charlotte spends with Jamie and Josephine in the orangerie. They sew and sing and take lunch. At two months old, Jamie's smile and personality blossom among the fragrant tropical blooms. When it is time for his naps, a cradle is brought in, and the baby naps under towering palms. All the while, Charlotte and Josephine exchange the stories of their lives.

One day, when Charlotte learns that Josephine was imprisoned for some months during the revolution, her face grows red.

"I suppose you think less of me now," Madam Bonaparte says, crisply stabbing her needle into her stitching.

"Oh, no, madam. On the contrary. To be falsely accused of something because of who a family member is…" Emotion lodges in Charlotte's throat. "It's unjust. But you endured. I'm more honored than ever to call you friend."

"Good. Because you will soon find yourself in more interesting company."

"Oh, madam." Charlotte looks at the palm branch directly above. "You tempt me to stay on indefinitely when I'm afraid I must be getting on."

"Getting on?"

"I came to France to find my husband's people only to find he struck out for military service because, in truth, he was very much alone in the world."

"And now you are alone in the world," Josephine says.

Charlotte peers down at Jamie asleep in his crib. "We are a pair."

"A woman alone, especially a young and beautiful woman such as yourself—no matter that she is a widow with a young one—will not escape the interest of men for long. Let me introduce you to some friends of mine.

"You're too kind to suggest such a thing. But I don't know, madam. I had hoped to find a small cottage in the countryside, somewhere far away from the intrigues of Paris, where the baby and I can build a quiet life."

"You must pardon me, then," Madam Bonaparte says, returning to her sewing. "I may have arranged for a small fête on Twelfth Night. You wouldn't want to disappoint me, would you, Madam Beaumont?"

"Of course not. I shall look forward to it," Charlotte says. "But then I must be getting on."

"Getting on? Whatever do you mean? You must stay just as long as you like. My husband and children are away so much of the time, and I truly enjoy your company, madam."

"You've been most gracious, but I am keen to set up my own household for me and Jamie."

"Where will you go? What will you do?"

Since sailing for France, Charlotte has had many weeks to contemplate what kind of a life she might make for herself and Jamie. Time and again, she's been drawn back to her boy's namesake and imagining what kind of life James would want for his son. She reasons that if James can't make that life for his son, then Charlotte might at least try.

"Perhaps grow a little something," she says. "I learned some things about sugar… I thought maybe I might find something similar."

"*La vie douce*. In the West Indies, it is sugar. Here in France, it is grapes."

Charlotte considers this. She knows nothing of growing and harvesting grapes, nothing of making wine.

"I should like you right here with me always," Josephine continues. "But if you must create a home for yourself, and I suppose I can grant that you someday must, you might consider Montmartre."

"Where is that?"

"It's a charming village overlooking Paris. In summer, their hillsides are lined with green grapes that make the most delicious Chardonnay."

"I don't think I should like to be that close to Paris," Charlotte says.

"Whyever not? All roads lead to Paris."

Keogh's Residence, Christiansted, St. Croix

Days after the new year, James sits with Keogh in the big man's drawing room, discussing the Countess of Tyrconnell's letter.

"You've been to the bank?" Keogh asks.

James nods. "It's a generous sum."

"So, you'll resume your search."

"I owe her that."

Keogh nods.

"But…"

"But?" Keogh urges when James doesn't continue.

"With harvest approaching and given my obligations at Seven Stars, I can't especially leave. I thought to start with a sizable reward of one hundred pounds."

Keogh laughs.

"You think it too much to start?" James asks.

"When Charlotte was kidnapped, you offered two hundred fifty pounds for her return."

"Two hundred fifty? That's a king's ransom!"

"It was," Keogh says. "But that's what she was worth to you."

James sits back and takes this in, yet another anecdote about the depth of his feelings for a woman he can't seem to remember. Eventually, he says, "I've already left notices at the dock. They should be in St. Martin in a week."

"Not wanted posters, I hope," Keogh says.

"No. 'The Countess of Tyrconnell seeks information regarding her niece, The Hon. Charlotte Dillon,' with her other aliases and a promise of a reward for giving credible information that leads to her whereabouts."

"How shall they get word to her?" the big man asks.

"They're to send word to me here."

Keogh smiles indulgently and shakes his head. "Charlotte doesn't know she has an aunt?"

"No."

"Then if she is still on St. Martin, she'll take one look at that notice and think it a lie."

"It isn't a lie."

"But she doesn't know that… and it may cause her to run."

Governor-General's Residence

For days, Lord Peter's mind turns over with the possibility that Charlotte Dillon could still be alive. He'd planned to introduce himself to Mr. Blair at the Twelfth Night masque. A social gathering, he thought, would grease the wheels for an eventual private meeting. Yet now that the masque looms this very evening, all Peter can feel is rage. How, he wonders, will he manage to chat up the man when he wants nothing more than to ring his neck?

Lord Peter watches the sun slide into the afternoon and, eventually, his frustration reaching a zenith, calls for a carriage. When the driver sets the wheels in motion, heading west out of town, the young lord strains at the window, peering ahead for some time. It's most unusual to call on someone without first sending a card. More unusual still to do so during an official holiday season, but Peter can't be bothered to care anymore. Finally, he sits back with a sigh, lets his head fall back on the squab, and fingers his flintlock.

Finally, the carriage wheels into the Seven Stars courtyard, stopping before the stairs to the great house.

At the front door, he knocks and O'Neil answers with a furrowed brow. When Peter gives his name, the butler asks, "Is Master Blair expecting you?"

"I should hope not," Peter says.

Taken aback by the open hostility, O'Neil crowds into the doorway, regarding the young lord skeptically.

"Aren't you going to invite me in?" Lord Peter asks, lifting his chin imperiously. "You wouldn't want word to get back to anyone that Master Blair is inhospitable."

"Any Irish gentleman worth his honor would understand that this is a holiday, and Master Blair is soon to leave for Christiansted."

Still Lord Peter does not move, nor does he seem in any way abashed. Eventually, O'Neil directs the young man into James's office, pours him a drink, and bids him to sit. "May I tell him what this is regarding?"

"No. I would have him intrigued."

O'Neil pauses by the door, tempted to throw the young lord out on his ear.

At James's dressing room, O'Neil knocks and is bidden enter. There he finds James with his valet, Hughes, putting the finishing touches on the planter's formal dresswear for the evening.

"Yes?" James asks.

"Sir, I beg your pardon. Belowstairs there is a young man—a lord, he claims—come all the way from Ireland to see you."

"He claims?"

"By his bearing and speech, he appears a gentleman. Lord Peter Fitzgibbon. But his manner…"

James narrows his gaze, thinking. "I don't recall seeing any such man's card."

"That's because he didn't send one, sir."

Hughes begins tying James's cravat, and James brushes him away. "He's come unannounced at Christmas?"

"I would be most happy to send him on his way for you."

"He's come all the way from Ireland to see me? What does he want?"

"He wouldn't say, sir. 'I would have him intrigued,' he said."

"Indeed, I am."

James strolls for the door, his snowy-white cravat still untied.

"I would caution you, sir," O'Neil says. "I get a very bad feeling about him."

James pauses and peers at his crusty butler, a man least likely to subscribe to feelings. Then he nods and goes down with O'Neil trailing close behind.

At the door to his office, James is just about to put his hand on the knob when the butler says, "Is your pistol still in your desk, sir?"

"Yes."

James enters his office and sees a boy with brown hair over soft features sipping an amber liquid. The young lord doesn't stand and doesn't smile. He merely regards him with searching gray-green eyes.

James can't help but smirk. He may have lost part of his memory, but one thing he knows for certain is that people with power rarely need to wield it while those who don't have it brandish its like any chance they get.

James strides to his guest. When he's towering over him, Lord Peter finally stands, and they shake hands.

"You'll pardon my dress, my lord," James begins. "I am shortly to leave for an engagement in Christiansted."

"We are to attend the same ball, sir."

"Are we?" James appraises Lord Peter and finally notices his formalwear. "Then you'll pardon my curiosity… This was something that couldn't wait?"

"I'm afraid not, Mr. Blair," the young lord says icily.

James sits behind his desk and eyes the drawer that holds his pistol. Then he regards Lord Peter, who remains standing, his fingers fidgeting on his glass and his gaze darting around the office. Again James looks at his drawer, then indicates for the young man to sit, and though Peter regards the chair overlong, he eventually does.

"You have me waiting with bated breath, my lord," James says. "State your business, please."

Peter imagined this moment dozens of times in recent months, imagined what he would say that would have the greatest impact. Yet now, his head hot with rage and his voice high, he says, "Charlotte Dillon. I know you transmuted her sentence to hang and she was spared to live here in this paradise."

James chortles. "You think this a paradise?"

"Compared to the hell she deserved? Yes, I do."

"Perhaps you might work a week in these fields. Drive the animals or stir the coppers. Perhaps you'd like to entertain some men at the House of L'Heureux."

"Don't be crude."

"This is what Charlotte did, none of it an idyll. My workers sign indentures to escape one fate for another. Who's to say which is worse?"

"I say."

"You say?"

Lord Peter nods emphatically.

"Tell me you didn't come all the way here to scold me for using indentures in place of slaves."

"I care not for the rest of them."

"Just her," James says.

"Where is she? And don't try to tell me she's dead. I know she isn't."

James sits back and shakes his head. Searching his mind, he recalls the name Peter in Charlotte's Crown file and goes to retrieve it. "What did you say your name was?"

"You'll not distract or dissuade me, sir."

Pulling the file, the book beside it slips out, and James absently collects them both, placing them on his desk.

"Your name," he urges, opening the Crown file.

The young lord stares eagle-eyed at the file and clenches his jaw. "Fitzgibbon. Lord Peter Fitzgibbon."

James spies the name in Charlotte's defense—according to her, this boy and his brother attempted to rape her. "The Lord Chancellor's son."

"His second son until Charlotte murdered my brother."

"Why did she murder him?" James asks, glaring at Peter.

The lord blushes and squirms. For so long he's clung to the lie that in moments like these, when he knows the fault lies so clearly in his weak hands, the heat of shame makes him feel small. Again Peter works his jaw. "I couldn't say," he utters.

"Couldn't or won't? Because it says here," James points with a flourish at the open file, "that your brother was trying to rape her. That you were helping."

"That's a dirty lie. Of course, she would say that. What would we want with the likes of her?"

"Rape doesn't have anything to do with desire, now does it? It's about power. Maybe you wanted to put that papist maid in her place."

Peter can't abide the blame wheeling around on him, so he says, "I'm told you had an affair with her."

"Who told you that?"

"Did you love her, or were you putting her in her place?"

Astonished, James suddenly considers that he doesn't know how he behaved with Charlotte in bed. He's always despised men who took women against their will. Always despised planters who used their slaves without a care for their consent. He knows his mind on these matters, yet Keogh has painted a picture of James with Charlotte that seems to imply he cared very little for propriety and honor when it came to her. For the first time in many weeks, James curses his impenetrable mind. "I can't say whether I loved her or not."

"She carries your child."

"No longer. That's certain."

"Where is she, Mr. Blair? She's escaped my justice for too long."

"My lord, if it were in my power to present her to you..." James pauses with his mouth ajar, for he was about to say, *I would*. Only a knowing voice inside says, *I would not*. This voice, this knowing, feels as though there once was a man who held Charlotte Dillon in his safe-keeping and, somewhere inside James, he still resides. In the end, it overrides all the man's caution. Hastily, James opens his desk drawer and grabs his pistol, weighing it to measure whether or not it's loaded. The heft lets him know it is.

James's heart is racing, and his mouth has gone dry when he says, "If it were in my power to present her to you, I would not."

Lord Peter brandishes a pistol, pointing it at James's chest, only to find that James has done the same.

"I was very much looking forward to the Twelfth Night masque," James says as casually as he dares. "I do not relish a ball of lead to the gut. I would imagine you feel the same?"

"In truth, I care very little for your desires, sir," Peter replies. "I want the girl, and you'll tell me where she is, or you'll go to hell with my lead in your gut."

Suddenly the door bursts open, and Peter, surprised, discharges his pistol. O'Neil, wide-eyed at the sharp crack of the gun, pulls his own trigger, and Peter jerks and falls to the ground. Racing for James, O'Neil finds him behind the desk, on the floor, eyes closing and blood spreading across his snowy-white waistcoat.

O'Neil calls for help, and in moments, he and the groom are lifting James and staggering for the hothouse. There, they place James on a bed, and O'Neil hurriedly explains to Juneh and Sisi about the gun shots and the other injured man.

After sending men to collect Lord Peter, O'Neil and Juneh strip James and uncover the bullet hole in his chest.

"His heart!" O'Neil cries. The butler, who's known James since he was a boy, has more than a devoted servant's tenderness for him.

Turning him, they see there is a clean exit wound nearer his shoulder.

"It miss Masteh Blaih's heart, sir," Juneh says.

"You're certain?"

Juneh nods. "I need to examine him. Can't say 'bout de lungs or ribs."

Moments later, the groom returns with another man bearing Lord Peter, and Juneh indicates a bed nearby.

"No," O'Neil says. "Master Blair will not open his eyes to see his crazed assailant in a bed across from him. Put him far from here."

"Dis de men's ward," Juneh says. "I can't put him wit' de women, and it be easieh fo' me to tend him heh."

"I care not whether it's easier to attend him," O'Neil says, indicating Lord Peter. Guilt at spurring the gunplay is eating him.

"I attend dem bot'," Juneh says.

"But you attend Master Blair first. Sisi can see to him," the butler says, indicating the young lord.

Juneh nods and turns back to James.

For long moments, O'Neil stands impotent, watching the nurses administer opium juice and clean the wounds. Every time he sees more blood running out of James's wound, every time he hears the planter moan, the butler feels the weight of guilt pressing down on him. What was he to do? he thinks. Behind the door, the words that were exchanged, he felt he had no choice but to act. Yet now, all O'Neil can see is the blood leaking out of James's chest and his skin growing ashen before the butler's eyes.

9

Château de Malmaison, France

When the sun goes down, torches are lit along garden paths from the château to the orangerie. Within, the potted palms and fruit that only a day before lay in neat rows are cleared to either side, making a lush tropical alley. Down the center, a long table—draped in white linen, strewn with rose petals, divided by floral sprays and bowls of grapes, and set with a gleaming gold service—sits beneath crystal candelabras. String musicians lean and sway into their instruments, playing lively waltzes, and soon guests in formalwear and wearing masks inspired by *commedia dell'arte* begin to arrive.

Charlotte, wearing a gifted gown and peacock-plumed mask, feels conspicuously like a pauper among princes—until one man appears at the door in full green-and-gold military regalia. He wears a plumed tricorn and a white mask with painted gold teardrops beneath his eyes, so there is nothing to be seen of his face. But beyond his striking green-and-gold formalwear and captivating mask, there is something about the man that draws Charlotte. Then his bronze eyes connect with hers, and she turns away.

While guests drink and mill and cat on about the glorious consul, about who's doing what in public and who's doing whom in private, Josephine devotes herself to one man in particular, a handsome hussar lieutenant many years her junior. No one seems particularly scandalized by this. In fact, they're deliberately indifferent. To Charlotte, there is nothing but fawning kindness. Guests politely inquire and enthuse about her, yet when she drifts away, their voices fall to whispers.

"Madam Bonaparte's newest pet."

"A colonial from her Antilles."

"What must they talk about?"

"Is there anything to that abominable place?"

"Sugar and slaves."

And all the while, the man in green hovers around them and snatches their conversations and, when Charlotte turns to him, nods.

Soon, platters—teeming with chicken and duck and salmon and venison in buttery sauces, beans and mushrooms and turnips, puff pastries and truffles and petit fours—are brought in, one after another, accompanied by towering tiers of glass goblets overflowing with champagne.

Madam Bonaparte clinks her glass, and conversation dims. "Dinner is served." With that, all the masks are removed, and when Charlotte moves to the table, the man in green takes the seat directly across from her.

Though refined enough to sit at this table, under Charlotte's scrutiny, she finds that he carries his arms wider at table than those around him. Uses his cutlery with less grace. Drinks with less restraint. And eventually, he looks squarely at Charlotte. "From whence do you hail, Madam Beaumont? Your French is flawless, but I think not France."

"I think you already know, sir. You've been hovering near to my conversations all evening."

The man grins, caught. "Ireland by way of the West Indies."

"And you, Monsieur…?"

"Heroux."

"I suspect your flawless French comes not from being reared here, Monsieur Heroux."

"You are correct enough, madam. I was dragged hither and yon by my parents, my father being a military surgeon. Raised but never rooted."

"Except, perhaps, in your father's military persuasion."

Heroux regards his military dress. "He taught me there are things worth fighting for."

"Worth dying for?" Charlotte adds.

"If necessary."

"You'll forgive me if I don't share your sentiments."

Heroux nods solemnly. "I heard about your husband. I am sorry, madam. That is the terrible price of these conflicts."

"So, you see why I am newly interested in peace."

"I am interested in peace, madam. Make no mistake. But I fear there can be no peace without justice."

Charlotte rearranges her napkin on her lap, fingers her cutlery for a moment, then traces around the rim of her goblet. All the while, the man in green watches. Finally, she looks at Heroux with a challenging gaze and says, "And who is to say what is justice?" Then Charlotte sighs, sips some champagne, and utters, "I'm so tired of all the fighting."

When the food is finally cleared, the music fades for cards and other games, including a guess-who game.

Heroux, his chocolate-brown hair handsomely askew and cheeks florid with champagne, chooses a name and slaps it to his forehead. "Living or dead?" he begins with a twinkle in his eye.

"Living," the rest say.

"Man or woman?"

"Man."

"French or not?"

"French."

"Libertine or puritan?"

"Puritan!" they shout and chortle.

Heroux frowns, then catches Charlotte's eye and smiles. "Royalist or Republican?"

"Republican."

The questions go on while Heroux narrows in. "Soldier or statesman?" he asks.

"Can one not be both, Monsieur Heroux?" Josephine asks while others answer, "Statesman."

"Indeed, one can, madam," Heroux replies. To the others he asks, "Am I loyal?"

A chorus of both yeses and noes and laughter is the reply.

"As you hear, monsieur, that depends," Madam Bonaparte says, "on whether one is loyal to his country or himself."

Heroux glances at Charlotte, then looks at Josephine. "Can one not be both, Madam Bonaparte?"

The First Consul's wife smiles slyly and says, "Indeed, one can."

Heroux indicates the name on his forehead. "Am I Tallyrand?"

"Yes!" the players clamor and clap.

Later, Madam Bonaparte corners Monsieur Heroux, and together they regard Charlotte. "I'm glad that you could make my little fête. I think my friend is quite amused by you."

"I was terribly glad to receive your invitation," he replies.

"I know the audience you prize. But whatever you do, monsieur, do not think to toy with her affections. I fear she is a tender lamb in a wolves' den here."

"I shall be as indifferent or kind as you require."

Josephine rolls her eyes at Heroux, and he smiles indulgently.

Seven Stars, St. Croix

James opens his eyes to a searing pain in his upper chest. His limbs are weak, and his mind cloudy, but as soon as a brown-skinned woman appears over him, smiling softly, and he knows who she is, he exhales. "Juneh."

Then Jenny's brown eyes and tight lips appear above him, and he blinks in confusion. "Miss Lund?"

James's voice is as weak as his body. He tries to take a greater breath, but his lungs burn and his ribs ache.

"You rest, Masteh Blaih," the nurse says. "Dat bullet graze you lung and broke a rib, but it go clean t'rough."

"How could you, Jamie?" Jenny asks.

"How, indeed," Mrs. Lund says, muscling her daughter out of the way so she can hover over James. Her high, blonde bun and ringlets frame a glower on her face. "What have you done, sir? Shooting my houseguest. What fine West Indian hospitality we offer here." She removes a handkerchief from her sleeve and waves it in front of her face. "The poor lord... Whatever shall I write his mother?"

Now James sifts through his mind and finds the memory, clear as day, of his confrontation with Peter. "Is he...?"

Juneh peers down the ward at a body taking up the far bed. "He live fo' now, sir. But he bad ailing. De bullet land inside his gut and still deh. You don't want be gut shot. It almost always kill ya."

A short time later, Keogh enters and pulls up a chair at James's bedside. "How do you feel?"

"Like I've been shot," James replies.

Moments later, Governor-General Lund enters, glancing at the young lord, then striding to James. "I'm glad to see you awake."

James tries to draw a deep breath, but his lungs burn and he coughs, and his lungs burn some more. "I wish I could say the same."

The governor-general looks at Keogh, then back to James. "There will have to be a formal inquiry."

Keogh sits back and clenches his jaw. "No need. The boy confronted Jamie with his flintlock at the ready."

"That may well be," Governor-General Lund says. "Still, I must serve the truth, whatever the cost." Glancing again at Lord Peter's bed, he says, "And he isn't a no-account."

"No, indeed. He isn't," Joanna Lund says from the boy's bedside before trumpeting her nose into her handkerchief.

Over the coming days, James convalesces while Keogh remains by his side, nursing and nagging and amusing. Though each laugh is an agony, it is a beautiful agony. After all, he's cheated death not once but twice in the past year.

When James eventually wanders over to Lord Peter's bed, he scrutinizes him. A youth of eighteen, young and full of promise, now almost certainly lies on his deathbed. The young lord's face is deathly pale and beaded with sweat. His mouth is dry and ajar, his breathing low and labored. *What a waste*, James thinks.

Finally, though it still pains him to breathe deeply, James returns on his own strength to his rooms in the great house. A short time later,

O'Neil arrives bearing a tray of food. The butler prepares James's place setting, then pauses, his gazed fixed determinedly on the floor.

"Yes?" James asks.

"Sir," O'Neil begins softly, "I would beg your forgiveness."

"Only tell me why and you shall have it."

Sheepishly, the butler looks up. "Do you remember the meeting?"

"I do, indeed. Perfectly."

At this, O'Neil's withers. "Then you know 'twas I who caused you to be shot. I'm so—"

James holds up his hand. "No, my good man, you did not." The butler opens his mouth to speak, but James continues, "No. The man who is responsible lies dying in the hothouse."

"But, sir—"

"No, O'Neil. I'll not hear it. Lord Peter came here with the intention of seeing me hurt, and 'twas he who pulled the trigger."

Still, the butler shakes his head while James nods.

"I beg you, think no more of it."

Reluctantly, O'Neil nods.

Marigot, St. Martin

Luci wends through the market with her daughters, Bella and Nicola, stopping at stall after stall to lean in and examine, to smell and marvel, to barter and buy. Until her eyes fall on a wall of tear sheets and one in particular with some conspicuous names:

> REWARD NOTICE
>
> The Countess of Tyrconnell seeks information regarding her niece, The Hon. Charlotte Dillon, also known as Charlotte Dillane, also known as Back from the Dead Red. If you have credible information that should lead to her whereabouts, you shall receive a sum of one hundred pounds, payable in gold.
>
> Intelligence should be sent to her agent in the West Indies,
>
> The Hon. James Blair, Seven Stars, St. Croix

Luci looks around, then tears the sheet from the wall and turns with the girls for home. Barreling into her kitchen, she calls for Nico, and when he strides in, she slaps the sheet to his chest.

Nico reads it, then gapes at Luci. "All this time I imagined he was looking for her. Haplessly, clearly, but that he was searching for her. We all assumed it, didn't we?"

Luci nods.

"Now he seeks her for this countess. Did she ever mention the Countess of Tyrconnell to you?"

Bent to preparing the noon meal, Luci merely shakes her head.

Nico huffs in astonishment. "She left for nothing. She set sail for France only a few months from giving birth, braving God knows what on the open water and Lord knows what overland to Paris. How could we have let her leave?"

Luci, chopping herbs, pauses to regard Nico. "She didn't exactly give us much of a choice, did she, love?"

"She didn't."

"You said it yourself," Luci says, tossing the herbs into a copper pot with coconut oil, "she's a determined woman."

"I did say that."

"Will you be the answer to this lady's prayers?" Luci asks.

"I don't know."

Seven Stars, St. Croix

Days after returning to the great house, James goes to his office to confront the scene. Yet there's no trace of the blood that should be there. Not even Lord Peter's glass. The only thing that remains is a dull ache in James's chest and the Crown file still lying open on his desk.

That's when James recalls that feeling he had while confronting Lord Peter. That knowing feeling that the man who loves Charlotte Dillon still resides inside him. When he woke from the gunshot with his memory of the incident intact, he thought—*he hoped*—that the effects of one traumatic injury might've erased the other. Yet now he glances again at the file and there's nothing.

James rubs his eyes. Then his gaze fixes on the model ship he built as a boy that so peculiarly resembles the *Anne*. Seeing that ship ignites a feeling of warmth inside his chest and makes him smile, and he stares at it until his eyes go dry.

Eventually, James ties the ribbon around Charlotte's file and picks it up to put away. Then his eyes fall on what was beneath the Crown file—*A Modest Proposal* by Jonathan Swift. Picking that up, too, he slides the Crown file back into its place on the shelf. But when James goes to replace *A Modest Proposal*, he finds the book doesn't close properly, and when he opens to the culprit, he finds a handkerchief on which his mother embroidered his initials. Fingering the delicate needlework, he smells a fragrance so familiar—primrose—that suddenly the empty caverns in his mind flood with memories and feelings of Charlotte.

James's knees buckle, and he collapses to the floor. At length, he sits, limp and overcome, clutching the handkerchief to his nose, breathing Charlotte in, and reliving it all—their meeting, her display at the House of L'Heureux, that summer day on the hilltop, their fight on the dock, making love, reading Juneh's note of Charlotte's pregnancy, every look and word and touch, all the fire and grief that made him the man he's been since that fateful fall day he met Charlotte. It's all there in his mind and heart now.

There's a perfunctory knock, then Keogh strides in. "Jamie?" Spying James, he rushes to him. "Are you all right? Are you in pain?"

James nods, for he is strangely in pain and all right.

"What's the matter?" Keogh says. "Can you breathe? Shall I call Juneh?"

"No."

"'No, you can't breathe,' or 'No, I shan't call Juneh'?"

"Charlotte." James peers up at Keogh.

Understanding, the big man smiles softly. "You remember."

Tears that had welled now fall in rivulets down James's face, and he nods. Never could he have known how numb he's been these past months in his forgetting if not for feeling everything so acutely now. Tender as a bruise, his heartache eventually turns to raw anger that compels him back to the hothouse.

In the men's ward, James spies Lord Peter, thinner, paler, and his breathing even more strained than when the James left. After a glance to assure himself no one is around, he pulls up a chair next to Peter's bed and whispers, "If I could have devised a suitable punishment for a powerful lord who would rape a powerless maid, no matter that he was a stupid, stupid boy, this, my lord, would be it. I wish you every agony on your way to hell."

Just then, Sisi enters the ward, and James smiles and fluffs Peter's pillow. Then he nods at the nurse and walks out.

Back in the great house, James finds Celine. "Tell Hughes to pack my sailing trunk."

"You going somewheh, Masteh Blaih?"

James gives his housekeeper a look that says the answer should be obvious.

Then O'Neil strides in. "You're leaving, sir? Do you think a trip wise at this point in your recovery? I wonder what Mr. Keogh would say."

But James merely turns on a heel and climbs the west stairs.

In his dressing room, James and Hughes have already begun to pack when Keogh strides in. "I hear you're leaving?" he says. "Good. I'll go with you, but you should wait."

"How can you say that?" James asks, pointing at certain shirts for Hughes. "You told me if I wait, I'll lose her."

"Months ago. A few days to secure your affairs to be away *and* to make sure you're well enough will make little difference now. And Lord Peter…"

"What about him?"

"You should wait until he takes his last breaths, which will be any day, perhaps any hour, now. See to his remains and write his family, then we'll leave."

James turns from his wardrobes to Keogh with a look of despair on his face. "What if she isn't on St. Martin?"

"You'll follow wherever she leads."

10

Three days later, Lord Peter Fitzgibbon finally breathes his last. With James's trunk already packed and the letter to the Earl and Countess of Clare written, he allows himself one grateful sigh, then stands and calls for his carriage.

At the dock in Christiansted, he makes arrangements for Lord Peter's remains and waits on Keogh. But just as the big man finally arrives so James can leave, a carriage bearing the governor-general rocks to a stop. He gets out accompanied by two barrel-chested men. Striding to James, he says, "Where are you dashing off to, sir?"

"An island jaunt," James says. "I should return in little more than a fortnight."

"Good," Lund says. "After all, I trust you have important affairs that tie you here. Still, I hope I may ask you a few questions before you leave."

"I would be happy to call my butler, O'Neil, for you. He was there and can attest to the man's murderous state."

"I should like to hear the man's testimony, but I should also like to hear yours before you depart this day."

James and Keogh exchange a calculating look.

"I'm afraid I must insist," the governor-general adds, and one of the brawny men brandishes some shackles.

For nearly two hours, James sits in the man's office, answering the same questions over and over. What was the stated purpose of Lord

Peter's visit? What was his demeanor? Where was his gun? Where was yours? Who wielded first? Who fired first? For the most part, James's answers remain exactly the same, though at times, his mind catches and his answers stray. In some moments, he wonders if the man isn't trying to deliberately lead him into greater blame, but finally, the governor-general sits back, satisfied.

When he escorts James to the door, he says, "I expect that Clare will require more." He looks doleful and *tsk*s. "His one remaining son…"

Château de Malmaison, France

After more than a month, Charlotte finally climbs into a carriage bound for Paris. But instead of returning to the abbey—Charlotte can't quiet her curiosity, can't stop imagining hillsides bursting with green grapes—she instructs the driver to bring her to the village of Montmartre.

North of Paris, the carriage climbs and climbs. High up on the butte, they wend past row upon row of brown vines that look like fields of crosses in a cemetery. And in the midst of those brown fields lie the crumbled ruins of the Royal Abbey, destroyed during the revolution.

Charlotte feels a pang of sadness at the destruction, a twinge of disappointment at the brown fields, for of course, at this very moment, Seven Stars is green and harvesting. Yet the windmill nearby makes her smile wide, and when she looks past the vines and the ruins, she can see that the hilltop is littered with them.

Near the ruins, Charlotte spies a tan house. "There, sir," she says to her driver. "Bring me there."

When the carriage stops, Charlotte steps down with the baby wrapped in a sling around her. There is some wind on the hilltop, and she wraps her cloak tightly around them, then turns to look down. Paris slopes far below, a cluster of buildings in the distance. Then she turns to the windmills and ranges her gaze far afield, imagining what it might look like bursting with leafy green grapes.

Then Charlotte goes to the house and knocks. For a long moment, there's no answer, and she presses her ear to the door, then knocks again. Eventually, footsteps sound, and the door is wrenched open with a creak. A woman in a black habit regards Charlotte skeptically, then smiles tenderly at the baby. "May I help you, madam?"

"I hope so, Sister. Do you own all this land?"

"It's what the state has left us, and we're grateful to have it. We don't want any trouble."

Charlotte nods. "Nor I, Sister, I promise you. I only wonder if I might buy a few parcels for my own. I have money and can pay what it's worth to you."

The nun peers around Charlotte to see an empty carriage and a driver waiting patiently. "Where is your husband, madam?"

"Lost in battle."

"You mean to seek the refuge of our order, then?"

"No. I mean to build a home and perhaps a vineyard, a modest one. Nothing to rival you, of course."

"I don't understand. You intend to strike out on your own?"

"I won't be alone, of course." Charlotte looks at baby Jamie.

The nun smiles kindly at the baby, then her countenance darkens. "You may apply to our order, but otherwise, I cannot help you. Good day to you." And with that, the door is closed in Charlotte's face.

Rankled, she climbs back into the carriage, and they set out for the village square.

There, they trundle slowly, looking for an inn or a bank, a shingle to indicate a land broker. All the while, the carriage with the conspicuous seal of the First Consul of France draws eyes to windows and people to doorways. They gape and point, yet Charlotte is undaunted. Montmartre, she believes, is ancient and majestic, scarred and tentative, but like the sleeping vines, it simmers with life just waiting to come back.

Eventually, they stop at an inn where the innkeeper's wife, Anouk Benoit, welcomes her and the baby with sturdy arms and a warm smile. The driver unloads their things in the largest suite the inn has, and Charlotte wanders to a window and peers out. The sun is slipping behind the caramel-colored buildings, and strangers are shuttering their windows, but there's something about this hamlet that strikes a familiar chord in her heart.

Marigot, St. Martin

In late January, the *Resolute* docks in Marigot, and James strides off, heading for the market. Amidst the crowded stalls, he feels as keen as he's ever been to find Charlotte. Yet he soon discovers that while little is known of her but the recent tear sheet, far more is known of the pirate Red, and the residents of Marigot begin painting different pictures of his whereabouts. Some say he went down with his ship while others say he returned months ago. Some believe him alive while others believe him a ghost. One thing they can agree on is that the pirate, if he is alive and on St. Martin, resides at his lagoon idyll—Belle Mina.

A spicemonger gives James detailed directions to the house, and with hope in his heart, James thanks the woman by buying all her cinnamon. Scanning the crowd for Keogh's bald head, James spies Luci, her hair as dark as night, her equally dark eyes fixed on him.

"Who seeks Charlotte Dillon?" she asks with a wary note in her voice.

No one James has met here has referred to her as Charlotte Dillon, and now his heart begins to race while he strolls to Luci. His voice is tight when he says, "I do, madam."

"For what purpose?"

"Merely to see her safely back to ones who love her."

"And if she does not wish to return?"

James looks down at the little girls, who are miniatures of their beautiful mother, and smiles wistfully. "She carries my child, madam. Or, at least, she did. Even if Charlotte should refuse me, I wish to know him."

"Or her," Luci adds.

James sees the image of a red-haired little girl, her chubby hand in his, beaming up at him, and smiles wider. "Or her."

Abruptly, Luci grabs her little girls and her basket, then turns and walks away.

Alarmed, James flags Keogh, then skips after her.

"Do you follow me, sir?"

"Where is she, madam?"

"My husband would not care to see me bringing home strange men."

"Is she at this Belle Mina I've heard about?"

But Luci merely walks on. Soon Keogh is keeping pace beside James, and while James keeps a distant eye on her, he explains to Keogh what he discovered.

A few blocks later, Luci slows as she approaches a gray stone house with blue shutters and iron scrollwork. Then the front door opens, and Nico points a rifle at James and Keogh. "That's far enough." Nico indicates for Luci to take the girls around back while the men stop with their hands up. "State your business."

"I'm looking for Charlotte Dillon," James says.

Nico smirks and shakes his head. "Perhaps I know where she is."

"Please, I don't mean you or your family any harm, I just—"

"And do you mean Charlotte harm?"

James peers around Nico, then up at the house. "Is she here?"

"No."

"But you know where she is."

"With whom am I speaking?"

"Oh, I-I'm sorry." James glances at the rifle and lowers his hands, introducing himself and Keogh. "Please, I swear I don't mean her any harm. I just—"

"You want the child, then," Nico says to James. "That's why you've come."

James glances again at the rifle. "May we please speak inside?"

Nico shrugs and invites them in.

When they're settled in the drawing room, James says, "I came for the child. I'd be lying if I said otherwise. But I want his mother equally as much." He feels a pang in his heart when he adds, "I love her."

At this, Luci slips into the doorway and asks, "Then why did it take you so long to come for her?"

Mortified, James looks at his lap and nods. "I should've come earlier, madam…"

"He suffered a wound to his head," Keogh says. "When he was searching for her, Jamie met a hurricane. Risked his own life to save his crew and ship. But he suffered a head wound that rendered all memory of some years, including everything he knew of Charlotte, all his feelings for her, lost to him."

"I was told of her," James says, "but it's one thing entirely to be told you love someone, altogether another to know it in one's heart. I'm ashamed to say that these past months, I didn't know what to do."

"And now you remember," Luci says, sitting down beside Nico.

"Now I remember," James says. "Please, if you know where I can find her, you must tell me."

Nico and Luci exchange a doleful look. Then Nico says, "She left five months ago."

"Left the island?"

"Left the West Indies."

Luci leaves.

"Bound for where?" James asks, his voice tight with fear.

Then Luci returns and hovers over James. "Swear that you love her. That you'll do right by her. On your honor, sir."

James peers up at her with a pleading look on his face. "On my honor, I swear."

Luci nods and gives him a slip of parchment. "There."

"Faire Abbey, Paris…" James's breath leaves him, and his heart sinks to his gut. "France?"

Nico and Luci nod.

"Why France?"

"She was determined to start a new life for herself," Nico says. "She feared you rejecting her and the babe."

"How could she think that?"

"I couldn't say," Nico says.

"You can't or you won't?"

"I can't. Though I tried, she wouldn't tell me."

James narrows his gaze at Nico, then looks at Luci.

"I vowed to kill you for her, but she wouldn't let me," Nico says.

"I suppose I should thank her, then," James replies.

"You should. I could kill you easily." Nico glances at Keogh. "Your man, too. I only say this to prove that Charlotte had no fear of your temper. And, in truth, I have failed her if she could not protect herself from you."

"Will I yet find her at this abbey? Is she intent on committing herself to God?" James is incredulous at that.

"No," Luci says. "She talked about a simple life in the country. I merely told her of Faire because I knew the nuns there would take her in and see her delivered of your babe. And I knew she could stay there as long as she needed."

"We have her destination." Keogh stands. "We thank you."

"Yes," James echoes, though he's still reeling.

When Nico follows them to the door, he adds, "If I should discover that you've been in any way cruel to her or the babe, I shall find you, sirs—both of you—and take great delight in killing you." He smiles broadly, tauntingly.

"Sir," James says, "if I should be so fortunate to find them, hurting them, I promise you, would be the last thing I'd do."

Montmartre, France

As days pass, Charlotte settles into Montmartre, depositing her money in a bank, creating a cozy temporary home for her and the baby at the inn, and exploring the vine-like village streets. At the residents who track her with their curious stares, she smiles warmly and greets them, but most only nod demurely, then look away. And no matter how much she searches and inquires, still a property remains elusive.

In early February, Charlotte is strolling toward a *boulangerie* when she spies an older boy deliberately thrust a foot out, tripping a woman. The woman stumbles to the ground, and her basket spills.

Charlotte rushes to help and glare after the boy. "Oh, madam, are you all right?" Then she looks around to see the other villagers deliberately walking on.

Charlotte, clutching Jamie in her wrap, helps the woman gather the contents of her basket and stand. Perplexed at the woman's treatment, Charlotte studies her.

Even shorter than Charlotte, Dinah Berger has a sun-worn face etched with sixty years of quiet endurance and silver hair trying valiantly to escape a kerchief.

"May I walk with you, madam?" Charlotte asks.

Madam Berger smiles cynically, then shakes her head. "You don't want to walk with me, madam. Folks are already suspicious of a woman come in a consul carriage. If you should be seen near me…"

"A consul carriage…?" Realization dawns. "My babe and I are no threat to these people, and I can scarcely think you would be either."

Now Madam Berger's smile is indulgent. "You would be surprised how small people's minds are. You must trust me, madam. You don't want to be around me."

Still, when Madam Berger walks on, Charlotte can't help but follow. Eventually, the older woman stops at the very last building before the village road gives way to fields. It is a modest, two-story ochre house with brown batten and shutters. At the front door, Dinah stops. "I know you follow me still, Madam Beaumont." Then she looks back at Charlotte. "I know what you want from me, but I'm afraid I cannot give it."

"How can you know what I want from you," Charlotte replies, "when I don't even know myself?" When Madam Berger doesn't reply, she continues. "What do I want from you, then?"

"You want what everyone wants. Something for which everyone despises me, and yet they need it all the same. Or perhaps they despise me precisely *because* they need it." The older woman puts a key in her door, saying, "I understand you want to buy land."

Charlotte strides to the door. "Have you some land to sell?"

Madam Berger invites Charlotte and the baby in, and when they are settled in the drawing room before a crackling fire, the older woman says, "I have some land, but it's not for sale."

"No?"

"No. One cannot buy land without money. That's why you're really here, isn't it? To obtain a loan?"

Charlotte sits back and looks around. Most French residences, she's discovered, have a crucifix hanging or a statue of the Virgin Mother. Not this one.

"You're a Jewess?"

Madam Berger nods.

"And do you practice usury?" Charlotte asks.

"Some believe it that. I believe the interest paltry, the very least I can afford to charge so I may live. I provide a service to these people as essential as their daily bread. I should be able to charge for it." Dinah smiles grimly. "They don't see it that way."

For a long moment, Charlotte stares into the cheery fire, then looks up at the low ceiling and roughhewn beams, the cozy furniture in the drawing room and the pair of polished silver candlesticks in the dining room beyond. It is a warm and inviting home, well kept, even loved, but it is hardly extravagant, not evidence of rapacious greed.

"I suppose you'll be leaving now," Madam Berger says.

"Would you like me to leave?" The older woman looks at her lap, and when she doesn't respond, Charlotte says, "Save the Bible, I've never known any Jews."

"The Jews crucified your lord, did we not?"

The woman's tone is crouched and defensive, and it suddenly occurs to Charlotte that in choosing France, she sought a country where Catholicism was not persecuted, yet there will always be other religions and people who are.

"Certainly not you, madam. And my Lord is a Jew. Some in the heat of a mob do not represent all, do they?"

Dinah shakes her head and smiles, and it isn't cynical but genuine.

"I don't need any money, madam. Will you keep a confidence?"

Madam Berger nods.

"I have enough money to buy more land than I could possibly require. What I don't have is a man to secure it."

"You mean to set up a home by yourself?"

"I can do it, madam. I am stronger and more capable than I might appear. Braver, too."

"You're here with me, so we already know that. But where is your husband?"

"Perished in the rebellion on Saint-Domingue." Charlotte has recounted this story so many times it almost feels real, and when she regards her sweet son, knowing that he'll never know his father, it brings tears to her eyes that she hurriedly wipes away.

Abashed, Charlotte regards Madam Berger, whose own eyes are glassy with tears.

"You loved him?" the older woman asks.

Charlotte nods.

Dinah's voice is thick with emotion when she says, "It is terrible to lose someone you love. Worse still, someone young, a man with the promise of life ahead of him. But worst of all, in war. Nothing seems to make sense. Some people are so keen to give their lives for a cause while others so eager to take advantage however they can. There will always be crows wheeling in the sky over carrion." Then she spits three times.

Charlotte furrows her brow in confusion.

"I suppose I *can* help you," the older woman says, standing and walking out of the room.

In an office, Madam Berger places some papers on a desk, sits, and regards baby Jamie wistfully. Then she indicates for Charlotte to pull a chair close and points at a crude rendering. "This is what I can give you. For a fair price, that is."

"Land?" Charlotte says.

"And a modest château."

"But I thought you said it wasn't for sale."

"It belonged to my son. He dreamed of being a vigneron, and when the restrictions against what positions Jews were allowed to hold were finally lifted, his father and I bought it for him."

"And you lost him during the revolution?"

Dinah tightens her trembling lower lip. "Not in the way you're imagining. Not in the way anyone should imagine. I wouldn't sell it to most people, you see, and no one from this village."

Charlotte waits, studying the grief and resentment written all over the older woman's face. Eventually, she says, "I'm honored you think me worthy."

"I suppose there's also the small matter that I haven't too many options from which to choose." They exchange a smile. "Do you want it?"

Charlotte nods just as the baby begins to squirm. "I should very much like to see it."

II

On the edge of a field of overgrown vines lies a one-and-a-half story buttercream-colored house with three hipped dormers under a sagging thatched roof. Batten wood shutters that once were blue are now weathered to gray, and brown vines choke the walls like gnarled hands.

For Dinah, the thrill of finally discovering a person to whom she may actually sell her son's farm has faded. The house appears now, as it has since that terrible day, like a stubborn wound that refuses to heal. Thrusting the key into the lock, she pauses for one heart-stopping moment, afraid of disturbing something sacred. Then she turns the key and leans into the door, shoving until it gives way and sending a whorl of dust into the air.

When it settles, Madam Berger notes that everything remains, though now shrouded beneath a thick layer of dust—the floors are red brick and the ceiling beamed. She watches Charlotte walk into the kitchen where a stone hearth dwarfs an entire wall, spider webs garland every corner overhead, and nests and droppings litter underfoot. Dinah feels the heat of shame singe her cheeks and opens her mouth to apologize, but Charlotte carefully, perhaps even reverently, climbs the stairs to the sleeping quarters.

Dinah shuffles into the drawing room and peels back a cover from a chair her husband carved with his own hands. Dragging a finger along a groove he made, she feels a stab of heartbreak. Then she returns the cover and goes upstairs.

There, the ceilings are sloped, and there's even more evidence of unwanted creatures. Charlotte stands at a mullioned dormer window, peering out at the gray-brown hills below.

"I suppose it isn't what you're looking for," Madam Berger says with some embarrassment.

Charlotte cradles Jamie's head and turns back to Dinah with a wide smile. "This is exactly what I'm looking for."

Lapine Inn

Meanwhile, in the village, a dashing young man named Robert Emmet enters the inn and hails the barkeep.

"Your usual room, monsieur?" Malo Benoit asks.

"Please. And tell your lovely wife I'd like whatever that heavenly aroma I smell is."

Moments later, his horse is stabled, his bags are delivered to a room upstairs, and stew steams before him. Emmet eats until he's nearly done, then looks to the barkeep. "I hear you have a new visitor in the village."

Malo looks to the goblet he's now drying with relish.

"A woman by the name of Madam Beaumont," Emmet presses, staring at the barkeep.

"I wouldn't know," Malo utters.

Finishing, Emmet stands. "Send word to my room when she returns."

Malo rests his hands on the bar, looks Emmet squarely in the eye, and sighs. "She's a young little madam with a newly born babe. I know better than to feed her to wolves like you."

"I think Madam Beaumont is not the lamb she appears. She may even be a wolf in sheep's clothing."

Malo shakes his bald head and waves his rag at Emmet. "You leave her be, Robbie. Plenty of better marks for your designs."

Emmet nods halfheartedly and turns for his room. What he keeps to himself is that he suspects there couldn't be a better mark than Madam Beaumont.

The sun is setting when Charlotte finally returns to the inn. After seeing to Jamie and freshening up, she returns to the dining room and strides to the bar.

"Monsieur Benoit, a round for the room on me."

A popular gathering place, the dining room has nearly two dozen people at assorted tables, and most cheer or nod their thanks.

"What are we celebrating, madam?" Malo says as he begins pouring.

"I am soon to leave here," Charlotte says, beaming.

The kindly barkeep frowns. "I'm sorry to hear that. I thought you were looking to settle in Montmartre."

"Oh, I am, monsieur. I am. I've purchased a charming little place to live, you see."

"Have you? Where will you be living?"

"Madam Berger had a property she wished to sell. A beautiful little place that needs only some love to restore it."

"Madam Berger? Do you mean Mathieu Berger's home?"

"Was that her son?"

"You don't want to live there, madam. It's almost certainly haunted."

"Haunted? Whatever do you mean? I saw the place. It is neglected, but I didn't see any ghosts."

The barkeep indicates for Charlotte to lean in, then he lowers his voice and says, "A terrible incident occurred there. Madam Berger is said to have cursed the villagers who did it. In truth, the whole village feels her contempt for it still. Some say she poisoned her well. Some believe the neighboring vines no longer produce the sweetest grapes, and no one knows the state of Mathieu's vines. Perhaps they are permanently soured."

"What happened, Monsieur Benoit?"

Just then, the barkeep's daughter, a chubby-cheeked girl of fourteen named Sidonie, emerges from the kitchen with her arms out. "May I hold him, Madam Beaumont?" She's always keen to cuddle the baby.

When Charlotte hands him over, the girl says, "I can hold him while you dine if you'd like."

Charlotte nods, and Sidonie heads to the kitchen with the baby, promising to return shortly with a meal. Charlotte takes a seat at the bar, and Malo beckons her closer.

"Have you seen the abbey ruins?" he begins.

Charlotte nods.

"'Twas a frightening time. Most Frenchmen are Catholic, and yet we despise the power and wealth we gave the Church. When the state took church lands, they offered them up to us to buy. Their coffers were bare, you see. Well, our coffers were bare, too. That's why we were revolting. Too many could scarcely afford to buy bread, let alone land.

"Jew bankers like the Bergers, they didn't need a church that refused them succor or a state that refused them citizenship. They just carried on being the middlemen between the powerful and the poor. That's where we placed them, and still we resented them for it.

"One night, some were all stirred up with envy and anger, went to their home with torches, and demanded our loans forgiven. There were angry shouts. Some were banging on doors and windows. Glass shattered. After warning them to leave many times, finally Monsieur Berger shot into the crowd. He killed a young man, but that weren't the end of it.

"The next night, a larger crowd, thirsty for revenge, sought their young son Mathieu at his farm. They stabbed him to death many times over and left his body for his poor *maman* to find.

"When she did, she tore the bodice of her dress and cried out such a mournful wail it could be heard across the hilltop. Then she cradled him in her arms until she fell asleep, and when she woke the next morning, she cursed the place, the whole village."

Astonished, Charlotte peers gape-mouthed at Benoit.

"It weren't right what they did that first night, but a belly full of nothing but bile can twist a man to do almost anything. What they did to Mathieu…" He shakes his head. "There's some anger still, some envy. Some even fear Madam Berger is a witch, but I think mostly it's shame people feel. I know I feel ashamed, and I weren't even there."

Moments later, the dashing young man with chocolate-brown hair and bronze eyes enters the dining room. He is arresting, and when Charlotte spies him, her eyes fly wide. "Monsieur Heroux, whatever brings you here?"

The barkeep, who only knows him as Robert Emmet, gives the young man a confused look, but Heroux smiles it away, takes a seat beside Charlotte, and says, "Would you believe I was looking for you?"

"Not for a minute."

Heroux chortles. "I hear congratulations are in order?"

"Yes."

The man raises his glass, and Charlotte does, too.

"What do you mean to do with it?"

"Settle here, of course."

"Of course." He regards her for a long moment, then asks, "Will you join me at my table?"

When they sit, they exchange small talk until their meals arrive, then the man asks, "Did you enjoy your stay at Malmaison?"

"I fear I overstayed my welcome."

"'Twas the opposite, I think."

Charlotte raises a questioning brow.

"Madam Bonaparte likes you, Madam Beaumont. Everyone could see it."

"She is most kind and gracious."

"She is a masterful judge of people and, in particular, men. I wonder very much what she thinks of me."

Charlotte muses. "You seemed to have a rapport with her."

"She is puzzling out my true intentions, and while she does, she has a particular appreciation for younger military men."

"I saw that."

"She's not shy about it. I wonder terribly what the general thinks. He is rumored to be quite devoted to her."

"I suppose I don't understand the ways of French women," she says.

"On that, we agree."

They carry on talking about Malmaison and the Bonapartes, the fête and its attendees, then he says, "May I call on you, madam?"

The abrupt change, the suggestion, renders Charlotte speechless.

"Am I correct in assuming you have no kin for me to petition?"

"I am my own woman." She pauses. "Of course, you may ask my son, but his opinions are mostly reserved to his needs."

Heroux chortles. "Men can be quite single-minded in that regard. I'm afraid it little changes as we age."

They share a chuckle.

For an unhurried moment, Charlotte regards the man. He is young like herself and most handsome. Still, a romantic entanglement is the very last thing she wants right now.

"I can see you're looking for a polite way of letting me down…"

"No."

Heroux nods. "I'm leaving on the morrow. Don't dash my hopes just yet. When I travel back this way, perhaps I might look in on you and your son?"

"I'd like that."

The next morning, Charlotte comes down the stairs with Jamie only to find herself in the midst of a loud argument playing out in the kitchen. Just as she looks to some patrons seated in the dining room for an explanation, Sidonie bursts through the kitchen door. "I'm not a little girl anymore. I'm going."

Charlotte peers at Malo, who stands in the doorway, then his wife, Anouk, who stands in the kitchen shaking her head. When Malo smiles reassuringly and shutters his eyes, Charlotte follows Sidonie outside to a brilliant blue sky and a subtle warmth that hints at the promise of the spring to come.

"May I ask what that was all about?" Charlotte says while they walk.

"Maman believes Madam Berger is a witch, but Papa told me I could go, and I want to go. I already adore little Jamie."

"And you do not believe Madam Berger is a witch?"

Sidonie shakes her head. "I am much more worldly than my maman."

Charlotte swallows a smile, and they carry on to the farm.

There, Madam Berger stands before the front door and hails them with a wave.

"Have you changed your mind?" Charlotte asks.

The older woman scrutinizes Sidonie for a moment, then looks at Charlotte and says, "I was worried *you* had changed your mind."

The night before, Charlotte lay awake musing over Monsieur Heroux's proposition, then imagining the terrible tragedy Monsieur Benoit recounted. By morning, Charlotte woke feeling determined. The property may be scarred, it may be neglected, but Charlotte is undaunted. As to Monsieur Heroux… She will consider him again if he ever returns.

"I've not changed my mind. In fact, I've already christened her."

"Have you?"

"I had a home once. 'Twas small and abandoned, but to me she was beautiful. In the end, I could not keep her, but I cannot forget her. Her name was Belle Mina. I should like to call this vineyard Belle Mina. If you don't mind, madam."

"Mind? I think it a beautiful name for a beautiful new chapter in her story. You may call her that if you call me by my name—Dinah."

Charlotte nods.

When she unlocks the door, she and Dinah enter with appraising eyes.

"I thought to start upstairs and work my way down," Charlotte says. "A good airing and scrubbing should give me a better picture of what needs repair and where. Do you mean to help me, Dinah?"

"If you'd allow. After I lost Mathieu, I locked away my grief here. I thought…" The older woman sighs. "I thought if you were giving her an airing, I might do the same."

Charlotte nods and remembers the baby in his sling, then looks to find Sidonie still standing at the doorstep, peering anxiously in.

"Have you changed your mind?"

"Madam, I…" The girl's voice is tremulous as she looks at Madam Berger. "I don't believe in ghosts."

"Neither do I," Charlotte says, her voice urging.

Sidonie looks at the older woman for a long moment, then sighs and steps tentatively inside.

Belle Mina

Over the coming days, the motley crew meets at Belle Mina for long days of labor. Charlotte and Dinah work in a cloud of dust, carting out all the furniture, sweeping away the cobwebs, cleaning the windows, scrubbing the hearths, polishing copper pans, beating rugs. Meanwhile, Sidonie coos and cuddles the baby, dangles toys before him, presents him to Charlotte to be fed, changes his napkins, and takes him for walks.

A week later, when the home is finally spotless, the cracks are laid bare. The roof needs repair, and some walls need repointing; some furniture needs to be replaced, and the well has gone bad. But when Charlotte inquires of men who might do the work, they merely shake their heads.

"You don't care for good coin?" she asks the third man who refuses.

Fleury Albert looks pained. He could use some good coin. He has nothing against Madam Beaumont. But how can he break the collective animus the village conceived against Madam Berger?

Monsieur Albert wipes his brow with his handkerchief and gives a tight shake of his head.

Charlotte glowers at the man. "Then you leave me no choice, monsieur. I must apprentice with you to apply the repairs myself."

"Oh, no, madam. I don't apprentice women. Only men should do such work."

"I smeared daub in the West Indies. Many women did. There is nothing to smearing that only a man may do."

Finally settled into her farmhouse, one Sunday afternoon near the end of February while the baby sleeps contentedly beside her, Charlotte sits at her desk and draws out her parchment and quill pot. At length, she stares out a window at the still-bleak fields, trying to fashion the proper sentiments. After all, a friendship with the First Consul of France's wife should be inconceivable. If not for their common knowledge of sugar planting and the West Indies, it surely would be.

Then there's a knock on her door. Charlotte peers out the window to see Monsieur Heroux standing on her doorstep, smoothing his hair, and her heart tumbles to her gut. Preoccupied with restoring Belle Mina, she nearly forgot all about the man's proposition.

Charlotte answers the door with a smile and a finger to her lips. "Jamie is napping," she says, leading him for a stroll around the house.

"I'm sorry for intruding, it's just… It's good to see you."

"And you, monsieur. What brings you to Montmartre?"

"You, madam."

The tone in his voice is so earnest, so fraught with something she can't quite comprehend, Charlotte stops and looks at Heroux. The sun shines brightly beyond his head, and she brings a shading hand above her brow to see him better. As handsome as ever, Charlotte determines any woman would be keen for the man's interest.

"I'm staying at Lapine," he continues. "I wonder if you and Jamie might meet me there for dinner this evening."

"Oh, that's very kind of you…"

"It's not a matter of kindness, madam. I assure you I would cherish it."

"You don't mind my bringing Jamie?"

"Not at all. I love wee ones."

"Very well. Then, of course, we shall be happy to come."

When Monsieur Heroux strolls back toward the village square, Charlotte returns to her writing. At length, she sits, struck by Monsieur Heroux's apparent interest. Eventually, she picks up her quill and writes to Josephine of her heartfelt appreciation for the woman's kindness and hospitality. She writes breezily of Jamie and Montmartre and Belle Mina, going on about the labor required to restore the farm and fields. Of Monsieur Heroux, she writes nothing.

Lapine Inn

That evening, Charlotte scarcely enters the dining room and requests a crib from Malo when Sidonie bursts through the kitchen door with her arms out.

"Sweetheart," Charlotte says to the girl, "I can have him with me while I eat. I do it all the time."

But Sidonie glances at the handsome Monsieur Heroux and insists.

At his table, Heroux stands and offers Charlotte a chair. Suddenly, she's struck with embarrassment and says, "She's always taking him for me."

"He is as irresistible as his mam."

Charlotte's cheeks flame, and she's never been so grateful for Malo when he appears to take their order. Charlotte and Heroux drink and talk at some length and, when the food arrives, eat and chat some more. It's mostly light and inconsequential until the man says, "Where in Ireland are you from?"

"A placed called Mayo."

A glimpse of something, perhaps recognition, perhaps something else, lights in the man's eyes. "Ah, that's a beautiful area."

"You know Ireland?"

"Some," Heroux replies. "It's a terrible shame... what's happened."

Remembering the man's fervency about justice, Charlotte stiffens and utters, "Yes." Her mind turns. "From whence do you hail, monsieur? I'm sorry I don't remember that you said."

"Here and there."

"But you lived in Ireland," Charlotte says. His easy use of words like *wee* and *mam* make her know this is so.

"For a time. I was sorry to leave it." Heroux regards her for a long, searching moment then says, "I can see I've disquieted you."

"Not at all."

But later that night, Charlotte lies awake, wondering about the mysterious Monsieur Heroux. He poses leading questions and remains evasive when it comes to answering hers. She has a nagging sense that he knows more of Ireland and its troubles than he's letting on, which makes Charlotte fear that he knows more of her than he's letting on. Yet maybe she is merely reading into things that aren't there. Maybe he's simply being solicitous. Josephine is probably right—no matter Charlotte's intent, a wealthy widow will draw the interest of suitors.

Heroux is kind and courteous, witty and handsome, and they have an easy rapport. He is precisely the kind of man with whom Charlotte might build a lasting friendship. All this she knows in her mind, and yet she can't seem to summon enough interest in her heart. At the end of the night, he brought her and Jamie home in his carriage and promised to call on them when he returned again to Montmartre. But she can't yet say she'll be glad of it.

Belle Mina

February turns to March, and all the while, Monsieur Albert's conscience plagues him. Until finally, early one morning, he collects Charlotte and takes her down the butte to the mines.

Just inside the cool, milky-smelling caves, they stop, and he lights his lamp. "Here is where we get gypsum to make lime mortar and plaster."

Once Fleury shows Charlotte how to load and pay, they return to his own home. There, they stand before a stone wall.

"First, clean out the joints with a hammer and chisel," the man instructs, then he proceeds to chisel out perfectly tuck-pointed lime mortar.

"Monsieur," Charlotte says, "you would ruin your own wall to show me when you might easily repair my own?"

After a pause, Monsieur Albert continues with a shake of his head, eventually sweeping away the mess and wiping the wall down with water. Then he mixes the lime mortar. "Now we let it slake. Don't overmix. Sit. We must be patient."

So, Charlotte reluctantly takes a seat the man offers. For what seems like an excruciating age, they sip tea and regard each other, exchange small talk about the weather and the village. Then Fleury mixes the mortar again and resumes his seat.

Eventually, he determines the mortar is ready to apply, scoops it up with a trowel, and butters the wall. He points and tucks and smooths with infinite care. Finally, the man stands back, beaming.

"You are an artist, Monsieur Albert," Charlotte says.

The man blushes and looks away. "Oh, no, madam. I am but a humble laborer."

"You construct buildings, monsieur? Homes, churches, stores? You restore what once was crumbling? Seems to me you build dreams. I can see plainly it is your calling, and I can scarcely imagine something for which one should feel more pride."

Charlotte looks at the man until he acknowledges her.

"I am most appreciative of your instruction. My home shall be the better for it." When Charlotte turns to leave, she adds, "Better still if you should gift it with your craftmanship."

Fleury watches the woman leave with a pang of regret. Never has anyone spoken of him and his work in such an admiring way. He'd taken up the trowel because his father and his father's father and so on had done so. There was never any thought but that he'd do it, too. Still, Monsieur Albert does love his work, he does believe it to be an art, and secretly he is proud. Perhaps Madam Beaumont was merely stroking his vanity to get him to work for her, but it didn't feel that way.

For some days, the man counts his meager coins, listens to his wife belittle him, and imagines how Madam Beaumont is doing with the walls of her château. Finally, in the middle of March, Fleury pats his salt-and-pepper hair and examines the lines on his face in a mirror. Then he straightens his shirt collar, takes up his tools, and heads for Belle Mina.

As he approaches the farm, he slows, suddenly anguished again with doubt about the property, about the legend of the curse, about Madam Berger. Then he hears a girl's chuckle and, cresting a ridge, spies the innkeeper's daughter dancing with a smiling and drooling baby. Monsieur Albert can't help but smile and strides on to the door, waving a good-morning to the girl.

"Madam Beaumont, is she…?"

"Inside."

Fleury knocks, and Madam Berger answers the door. Struck with unease, he remains on the doorstep, his mouth ajar to speak, but nothing comes out.

Eventually, Dinah says, "Have you come for Madam Beaumont?"

"Y-yes, madam." The man cranes his neck to look inside while remaining firmly outside. "Is she here?"

Madam Berger opens the door wide and steps back. Still her face is flat, her body tight.

"Perhaps this was a mistake," Fleury says, turning to leave.

"Monsieur," Dinah says, sighing. "Madam Beaumont needs your help. If I must leave for you to help her, I shall. Only do help her. She's up the stairs."

The man turns back, and at length, Fleury and Dinah regard each other. Monsieur Albert has convinced himself he is merely helping a kind young widow. That is all. But, in truth, the murder that occurred on this very doorstep eight years before still torments him even now. He could say he was brash and unthinking then. Yet at thirty-six he was no callow youth. He could say he was swept up in the mob. That he was poor. Yet they were all poor, and they didn't all act.

In truth, he's turned away from Madam Berger not because of her shame, but because of his. He never thrust a blade. Still, he's carried the guilt of hurling anger and slurs all these years. Perhaps now, somehow, Fleury Albert can find a way to make amends.

"I can help her," he says, "if you'll let me."

12

Faire Abbey, Paris

*I*n early April, the carriage bearing James and Keogh finally stops outside the abbey. James's heart pounds in anticipation while he peers up at the august buildings. Then he looks to his friend and opens the carriage door.

At the massive doors, James knocks and, after a long wait, one swings open. A woman in black habit and gold pectoral cross stands before him, her gray eyes narrowed skeptically.

"Madam—"

"Mother Abbess," she corrects.

"I-I'm sorry. Mother Abbess—"

"Do you not speak French here in France, monsieur?"

Thankfully, the abbess speaks English well, but her consternation at James's improper address, then his language… He blushes, chagrined. "I can try, but it doesn't come easily to me."

The abbess heaves a great sigh, then purses her lips.

"I am searching for someone, a woman very dear to me, and her baby. *My* baby. Charlotte Dillon is her name."

"There is no one here by that name."

The abbess steps back and attempts to close the door when James jams a foot in. "Please, Mother Abbess, I have sailed all the way from the West Indies, and I know she came here." The woman's face softens ever so slightly, and he adds, "Please."

The abbess looks at Keogh. "This is a sanctuary for women and girls." She wags a finger and says, "Your tough remains in the carriage."

James regards Keogh. "He isn't a brute—"

"I'm happy to remain at the carriage," Keogh says.

Through the garden and hallways, James cranes his neck to look around, hoping against hope that he might catch a glimpse of Charlotte, that after all this, finding her might be that simple. But eventually the abbess directs him into her office. Sunlight shines through stained glass, painting the woman's desk in shades of purple and red, and lamps flicker with low light.

When the abbess sits, she regards James with suspicion. After more than a dozen years as the head of the abbey, she's interviewed hundreds of men, mostly fathers enrolling their daughters in the abbey, but dozens of husbands, too, seeking to retrieve their wives. This man, broad and beguilingly handsome, would be the precise disguise the devil himself would use, so the abbess steels herself. "Your name, sir?"

"James Blair."

The abbess knows very well she had a resident come from the West Indies by the name of Charlotte and is all but certain she bore a son that she called Jamie. The abbess also knows there are two types of women who flee their husbands: one who intends never to return and the other who allows she'll likely return. The former is not likely to name her son for a man she fears. Still, in this ministry, the abbess cannot be too careful.

"And you're searching for this woman... why?"

For a long moment, James stares and grapples, then says, "I love her."

In all the impassioned pleas the abbess has heard over the years, surprisingly, this is an unusual one. Rarer still is the tone in his voice, so small but certainly there—that of heart-wrenching vulnerability.

"And does she return this sentiment?"

Without hesitation, James says, "Yes."

The abbess is not the sentimental type. In this ministry of protecting women from cunning abusers, she cannot afford to be. Still, her crusty heart can be moved, and some men can be redeemed. Sitting forward, she threads her fingers together, and smiles dolefully at James. "This abbey exists, in part, to provide refuge for women and children to escape untenable relationships. Forced marriages, abusive husbands, fathers, brothers, even sons who would place a woman in an arrangement against her will. Which are you, monsieur?"

"Mother Abbess, I am ashamed that there should need to be places such as this for women and children, yet I am grateful, too. That you were here for Charlotte when she needed it. But I swear to you she need have no fear of me. In her heart, she knows this, too."

"You'll forgive me, given my position, if I am dubious, monsieur."

James nods. "I do understand—"

"This woman is your…?"

He gulps. "Legally, she was my indenture, but I promise you," he rushes on, "she is far more than that to me. She knows this. In her heart, she does. And I swear to you, I shall remedy that arrangement at the nearest opportunity."

The woman shakes her head. The indenture status makes her bristle. "You love her, and she loves you? She is far more than an indenture to you and knows this? Why, then, should she flee and so far at that?"

"I want desperately to know the answer to that myself."

"You'll grant, monsieur, there is a gap in your story."

James nods.

"It is around these gaps where I nose." At length, the abbess scrutinizes James, then says, "I can give you nothing today."

"Pardon me?"

She slides forward a parchment and quill pot. "If you'd like my help in locating this Charlotte Dillon, you'll give me your particulars—name, place of residence, position. Leave nothing out that can help me measure the veracity of your claim. You may return no earlier than one month from today to inquire as to the progress of my investigation…"

"One month!"

"At the earliest, monsieur. In truth, given you've come from the West Indies, it may take me as long as four or six months to secure an accurate impression of your character."

"Six months! Mother Abbess, please, I shall be happy to tell you anything you need, only tell me she's here. Tell me where I can find her, I beg you—"

But she holds up a hand, undaunted. "Monsieur, many is the man, earnest and desperate as you, painting a picture of love and safety in this office as you, who is nothing but abusive and cruel beyond the gates of this abbey. I would not be ministering to my ladies if I neglected them for a pretty man's pretty words."

James shakes his head, and the abbess indicates the parchment and quill. Taking them in hand, he scribbles a name. "You must write my mother in Ireland."

The abbess smirks. "A mother's love is blind. Will she not write me that you are precious?"

James regards the abbess with frustration, then scratches his mother's name out. "The man you bid stay at the carriage," he says, writing Keogh's details.

"Your hired tough? Do you not pay him to protect you?"

"He is not my hired tough but a true friend. If anyone knows my character, it is he."

The abbess weighs this, then gives a tight nod and adds, "But I'd also like the word of a man who has reason to dislike you."

James shrugs petulantly. "Then I can give you nothing, for I am well loved by everyone who knows me." He exchanges a smirk with the abbess. "In truth, there are many who despise me on St. Croix, but only because I am not cruel enough." Then he writes another name and slides it forward. "If you must write to St. Croix, you should write my former slave. If anyone knows cruelty and kindness, if anyone can measure a man, it is she."

The abbess considers this, then gives another tight nod and ushers James to the door.

"At least tell me about the baby. I'm told Charlotte was due to be delivered around the end of October. She must've given birth here. Can you not tell me if she survived it? If the baby lives?"

"I cannot tell you about Charlotte Dillon, but I *can* tell you that no woman or baby has perished in this abbey in the past year. Now…" She opens the door. "One month, monsieur, and I may have some more information for you. In the meantime, you must call on God for patience."

For James, his feet feel like lead weights as he shuffles reluctantly down the hall behind the abbess, looking in every open door, peering up every staircase, his throat painfully tight for suppressing the urge to call out to Charlotte.

Eventually, the massive doors at the main gate are closed behind him, and James stands on the outside, aghast. Never did he imagine traveling all this way only to be stopped in his search by an imperious abbess. His heart is aching when Keogh strides down the street towards him.

"Well?" the big man asks.

James shakes his head. He has no words for how incredible this all seems. "They're protecting her. We have to wait."

Belle Mina, Montmartre

The once-abandoned vineyard is now bustling with people. Charlotte and Dinah and Sidonie and Jamie are nearly always there. And Monsieur Albert has enlisted a man to restore the well and another the roof.

Now, in the middle of April, Charlotte stands with another man Fleury recruited. Lazare Gérard is nearly seventy years old with wild white hair and a bushy white beard. He has kind, glacial-blue eyes that crinkle warmly when he smiles, though he isn't smiling now. The older man removes his hat and scratches his forehead, looking gravely down at the vines.

"They're badly overgrown," Lazare says.

"It's hopeless?" Charlotte asks.

The older man traces a reverential hand up a tan shoot amidst gray-brown bark. "Neglected, some say cursed. Still, the sap is rising." A tender smile spreads on his face. "Some things refuse to die, no matter what we do. No, Madam Beaumont. Nothing is hopeless."

Then Monsieur Gérard gets down on his hands and knees and grips a trunk. "We go back to the beginning when the vine held its promise. Then we choose our cane."

"Cane?" Charlotte squats, now more intrigued.

"See these arms?" the old man says, indicating bark that spreads off from the trunk. "These were once tender shoots that bore fruit. Now they are the arms that lead to more shoots. We call them cane."

For the first time in many weeks, Charlotte feels an ache in her heart for James, and tears well in her eyes. Monsieur Gérard regards her curiously, and she quickly knuckles them away.

"We need to choose our shoots to create new cane," he continues. "Then we tie them to the horizon and wait for bud break."

"Tie them to the horizon?"

"So the new shoots can reach for the sun."

Monsieur Gérard stands and surveys the fields, and Charlotte does, too. Finally, he says, "'Twill be some hard work to ready these vines for bud break."

"I have done hard work, monsieur. I'm not afraid." And she isn't. Strangely, Charlotte is keen for it. To have something she can prove to James, that she can raise their son to be a planter. Perhaps more important, she would prove it to herself.

"Then I'll be back at sunrise," Lazare says.

And, indeed, he is. The next morning, when Charlotte crests a ridge to the vine rows, she stops. There Monsieur Gérard is already bent to a vine, pruning and shaping and tying. Down the next row stands a boy of thirteen. Wiry and determined, he regards his tangled vine like a cherished puzzle he would solve, then clumsily he does his own pruning and shaping and tying.

"Monsieur!" Charlotte calls out.

The old man and the boy look up, then Lazare waves her over to the end vine of another row. "Do you remember what I told you?" he asks.

"Go back to the beginning," she says, grasping the trunk, "and find its promise."

Lazare helps her to feel the vine. "There's life where it bends, you see."

Charlotte nods and chooses her shoots, then prunes, every clench and cut requiring more strength than she imagined it would.

"Careful," Monsieur Gérard says while she shapes. "Careful."

After only one vine is done, Charlotte stands and peers down at her sore hands, then ranges over the neglected field of vines and lands again on the boy still working feverishly. For the first time, she can appreciate the immense responsibility James has at Seven Stars. Yes, in the end, that is his cane and his profit, but he must care for a village of people with it. Then Charlotte feels a tremendous stab of regret at her privateering. Now she knows it was never as simple a calculation as Madge depicted. They didn't just steal from James—they stole from Shea and Aoife, from everyone who worked those cane pieces.

"Can you manage?" Monsieur Gérard asks, jarring Charlotte from her musing.

She straightens and beams. "Yes."

Over the coming days, Charlotte wakes before the sun, dresses by feel, feeds and cares for the baby until Sidonie or Dinah arrives to care for him, then strides off for the fields, her hands growing callused working her own twisted vines. A week passes, and one day the boy, whose name is Geoffrey Moreau, is joined by his twin Georges. Each spurred on to best his brother, they work keen and fast.

One morning, when April turns to May and the giant task of spring pruning is nearly done, Charlotte spies a shadow fall across the vine on which she's working. She looks up to see a woman with ash-blonde hair and steel-blue eyes glowering at her.

"May I help you?" Charlotte asks.

"What do you think you're doing here?" the woman asks.

"Pardon me?"

Charlotte peers across the rows to Lazare. The old man has stopped his work and regards the pair of women with narrowed eyes.

"The Jewess cursed these vines, and if she didn't, I cursed them." She spits on the vine, and Lazare calls out, rushing as fast as his old joints can carry him.

Monsieur Gérard arrives breathless at the vine and asks, "What are you doing here, Madam Faucher?"

"I could ask you the same, monsieur."

"We're pruning away all the dead vines so the new shoots can breathe again."

Béatrix Faucher purses her lips. "I know what you're doing. I only meant, why are you doing it here?"

"Can you imagine a better field for such work?" the old man asks.

Color floods into Madam Faucher's cheeks. Her eyes glisten, and she clenches her jaw. Then she turns on a heel and walks away.

When the woman is nearly out of sight, Charlotte asks, "What was all that?"

"Sometimes it is people who must let go of dead things so they may breathe again." And with that, Lazare returns to his vines.

The very next day, Monsieur Heroux returns. Holding six-month-old Jamie on her hip, Charlotte feels a confused mix of delight and wariness while she watches the man alight from his carriage. Opening the front door, she greets him with a warm smile that he returns. His sun-kissed face and tousled brown hair make him even more handsome than she remembers. Her heart should be leaping, but it isn't. Charlotte knows she should politely send the man on his way with gratitude for his kindness. She might even explain that her grief over her lost love is still strong, which is true. It's then she is struck by Monsieur Gérard's wise words about letting go of dead things.

"Won't you join us, monsieur?" she asks. "We were just about to eat the noon meal and have plenty to share."

"I would be delighted to."

They sit down to duck *cassoulet*, Charlotte apologizing all the while for the state of her hearth, her dining table, even her food-smudged son. Finally, Monsieur Heroux presses his hand calmly to hers and says, "It's lovely, madam. I promise you I like you just as you are, or I wouldn't be here."

The handsome man gives her a searing look that she knows should make her blood race, but conspicuously, it doesn't.

After lunch, they take the baby on a walk, talking of Josephine and Malmaison, of Montmartre and grapes. When they turn to walk back, Monsieur Heroux says, "Have you no wish to return to Ireland?"

"No," Charlotte replies without hesitation.

"That was… unequivocal," he says, and they exchange a chortle. "I have often thought of returning."

"Have you?"

"I feel compelled to do what little I can to help."

"Help in what way?"

"I'm incapable of allowing an injustice to carry on without doing something to remedy it. I am in awe of those brave souls who fight for a free Ireland."

Suddenly, Charlotte feels exposed, and her heart races as she says, "You know of that struggle?"

Heroux nods. "In particular, I am inspired by a young woman by the name of Dillon. Her father, Lord Charles Dillon, was a powerful orator who spoke passionately for the rights of his people and for a republic of Ireland. You're from Mayo as he was. You must surely know of him, madam."

"I've heard the name," she utters.

"He died before the Crown could arrest him, but he had a daughter. She would be about your age now, but when she was only seventeen, she assassinated the Lord Chancellor's son. Some believe she died before they could hang her, a nonsense about a brawl turned deadly, but many don't credit it. We believe she escaped to the West Indies and turned pirate for the cause. Called herself Back from the Dead Red because of her vivid red hair. Hair just like yours, in fact. Some believe she went down with her ship, but many don't credit that either. We believe she's fled the law a second time just waiting for the right opportunity to fight for the cause again. Living in the West Indies, being from Mayo, surely you've heard of her exploits."

Charlotte's throat has gone tight and her mouth dry as ash when she says, "That sounds like a fairy tale, monsieur."

"I assure you she is very real. A privateer who plundered dozens of Proty ships. Some of these proceeds made their way back to Ireland, but some are lost." He turns and regards the hill of vine rows. "I do wonder what became of her and her gold. She would make an invaluable ally."

Hearing her feats recounted back to her, Charlotte is paralyzed with uncertainty. Heroux's tone is so assured, his allusions so casual, he must certainly be baiting her. Gratefully, Jamie begins to fuss, and she makes an excuse to tend to him, turning back for the house with long strides. When eventually they approach, she says, "It seems you have a valliant interest in Ireland's fate."

"I confess, I do, madam. And you."

At the front door, Charlotte stops. Now she feels all but certain his interest in her is in the cause of justice and not romance. Unwilling to be dragged back into Ireland's turmoil, she turns to Heroux and says, "I wish you luck, monsieur. I sincerely do. They will need all the help they can get."

Monsieur Heroux nods, even as he fidgets and scrutinizes her. "I hope I haven't overstepped."

"Not at all," she says. "It's only that in my simple life I must attend to domestic things. You can see I haven't the comfort to be so principled."

"May I call on you again?"

No. This is what Charlotte desperately wants to say, but instead she demurs politely, "If you'd like."

Monsieur Heroux nods with a tender smile. Turning for his carriage, he calls out, "It isn't luck we need, Madam Beaumont."

That night, Charlotte lies awake, wondering how it could be that Monsieur Heroux—if that is even his name; now she isn't so certain—discovered her true identity. Wondering what he truly wants from her and whether money will be enough. If there was a part of her that thought intriguing on behalf of Ireland would be in her future, now with the opportunity laid before her, Charlotte knows she wants no part of it. And this handsome man, whether his cause is noble or not, is not James. He does not stir her like James. And he never could.

13

Faire Abbey, Paris

Exactly one month to the day after James's last visit, he arrives again at the abbey. But this time, the abbess stands at the main gate door and shakes her head, refusing even to invite him in.

"But you said one month, and it's been a month. Can you not tell me anything? Please?"

"I can tell you, Monsieur Blair, that I have done what you requested. I have written your slave Juneh as well as the governor-general on St. Croix. If delivery—"

"The governor-general?"

She nods. "I thought he would be in a fair position to speak to your character as a man."

James's mouth gapes. With Jenny and then Lord Peter, Governor-General Lund can scarcely be expected to be fair.

"If delivery is true," the abbess continues, "we can expect replies in early September. Now we wait."

Yet once again, when the abbess goes to close the door, James wedges it open with a foot. The abbess peers down at his foot and pulls her lips into a tight line.

"You deliver women from abusive arrangements," James says, "but you do *not* deliver them from their babes. Won't you at least tell me where she was delivered?"

"Again, monsieur, I cannot tell you of Charlotte Dillon, but I can tell you our ladies generally deliver at the Hôtel-Dieu."

The abbess looks down at James's foot.

"Won't you please speak with my friend John Keogh?"

The abbess looks at Keogh, who, upon hearing his name, hovers now directly behind James. At length, the woman considers this, then looks at James. "You may return with Mr. Keogh in August. Perhaps by then I shall have heard back from St. Croix. And, if not, I shall lend some consideration to what your friend has to say on your honor."

From there, James and Keogh go directly to the Hôtel-Dieu. At James's request for information, they are led into an office and, a short time later, Madam Lachapelle strides in and sits.

"I am told I should seek the head of obstetrics," James says.

"You have found her," Madam Lachapelle says irritably.

The woman, with her air of authority and unlined face, brown gown and ruffled collar, is a mass of contradictions, and James and Keogh exchange a look of surprise.

"I seek a woman," James begins. "I understand she was a patient here."

"We have many women patients here, monsieur. Can you be more specific?"

"She would've been delivered in October, likely late October. Her name is Charlotte Dillon, and she has vivid red hair."

Madam Lachapelle frowns, searching her memory. "I do recall the hair. She was a little madam. 'Twas a difficult labor."

"A-a difficult labor?" James asks, his heart in his throat.

The woman goes to her files and searches through them. "What do you want with her?"

"Any details you can tell me. An address, perhaps."

"Many of our patients are indigent. We treat them regardless of address or coin. Ah, yes." Madam Lachapelle pulls a file and scans it, then frowns and *tsk*s. "No. This Charlotte is not Charlotte Dillon. I'm sorry, monsieurs."

James cranes his neck to peek at the file, but the woman pulls it away.

"You have a Charlotte who delivered here in late October?" he asks.

"But her name was not Dillon."

"Did she, by chance, reside at Faire Abbey?" James asks.

Madam Lachapelle glances at the file, then scrutinizes the pair. "What did you say you want with her?"

James's shoulders slump, and his face falls.

"I have no information on Charlotte Dillon," she continues. "I may know of another Charlotte, but it is so difficult for me to keep accurate records. What with all the destitute we treat, fencing against all manner of calamity, all the time I must spend seeking funds simply to stay open." Madam Lachapelle peers pointedly at James.

"I would be only too happy to make a donation," James says.

"How kind you are, monsieur. We would be so grateful for your generous donation." The woman looks again at her file. "I can tell you Charlotte *Beaumont* was delivered of her babe on the twenty-fifth of October. 'Twas she who had vivid red hair. Now perhaps she is not who you seek, but—"

"Beaumont?" James asks.

The woman nods.

"And you said it was a difficult labor. Is she well recovered?"

"She left our care in rude health."

"And the babe?"

"Lusty and strong."

"Girl? Boy?"

Madam Lachapelle looks once more at the file. "A boy. Christened James."

Emotion burrows up through James's throat and wells in his eyes. "A boy," he says, breathless.

Belle Mina, Montmartre

In early June, the air warms and the shoots flower. After Monsieur Gérard directs his crew through the vineyard, cutting away the shoots that remained as security against frost, he leads them through a delicate hand-pruning of each vine. While this step is time-consuming and laborious and the boys groaned when Lazare announced it, to Charlotte, it is anything but tedious.

Monsieur Gérard stays by her side for the first row, inspecting each vine, teaching her about each tender shoot, what should stay and what, for the health of the vine, should be plucked away.

"Too close," he mutters, picking one shoot away, then another.

Charlotte narrows her gaze, confused. "How do you know which to keep and which to pluck away? Those seemed as good as any other," she says, indicating the discarded shoots on the ground.

"Space, madam," Lazare says. "Some you keep and some you must discard. You're just learning, but in time you will know in your bones, in your heart. 'Twill be like breathing. You won't even have to think about it, what makes the sweetest grapes."

"'Twill be an instinct," Charlotte says.

"Yes."

"Do you think…" Charlotte pauses, and heat floods into her cheeks. "Do you ever think that our instincts may fail us?"

Monsieur Gérard scoffs and scratches his head. "I'm no mystic, madam. Merely an old vigneron."

"That's precisely why I ask you, monsieur."

Lazare peers at the vine. "I think our instincts are never wrong. The only thing that's wrong is when we mistake something else for them." He indicates the vine. "Then we pluck the wrong shoot."

A robin calls, arms creak from nearby windmills, and the air is warm and sweet. All the while, Charlotte muses on the dream that compelled her to flee the West Indies. Time and again, she has gone back to that feeling of wanting so desperately to be close to James. That longing made her leave, and now she can't tell which was the instinct—to love him or to leave him.

"What if I should pluck the wrong shoot?"

"As long as a healthy trunk remains, you can fix it."

Back to work Monsieur Gérard goes, bending his head and narrowing his gaze, fingering the shoots and cradling the flowers. All the while, his eyes shine with love. It is a thing of beauty to see the old man work, and many are the times when Charlotte is caught regarding him and not the vine.

In the waning days of July, Monsieur Heroux returns. Charlotte sighs at the man's persistence. After some weeks, then months, passed, she had hoped he'd received the message in her subtle tone. Apparently, he hadn't.

"Do you suppose he will ask you to marry him?" a dewy-eyed Sidonie asks with a blush flooding into her cheeks.

"I hope not," Charlotte replies, handing Jamie to her and opening the door. "Monsieur Heroux, what a pleasant surprise."

"Madam Beaumont, seeing your beauty, I am reminded what a fool I've been to stay away."

Charlotte leads him out to a secluded trail. "I think you a man of great industry who's been devoting himself to more important things than an insignificant vigneron in Montmartre."

"I promise there is nothing insignificant about you."

"You're too kind to me. And because of your kindness, I find I must now speak with candor. Whither you seek a friend, you have it. As to something more, I am not free. Though he is gone, my heart is still bound to Jamie's father. I'm sorry if you were hoping for something more."

Heroux nods. "Though my heart is breaking, I supposed as much."

Charlotte smiles indulgently. "Somehow I suspect you're a man who devotes his heart to greater loves than me."

"I do have a great love. Something I have loved as much as any woman. I wonder if you aren't the very person to help me with that."

Of course, I shall help you if I can. That is the polite thing for Charlotte to say. Her mouth gapes with it, and still she can't bring herself to say it.

Monsieur Heroux's eyes dart furtively around them, then he whispers, "I wonder very much if you have ever gone by a different name than Madam Beaumont..." When Charlotte doesn't answer, he adds, "Just as I go by a different name."

"What do you want from me, monsieur? I beg you, state your business plainly."

"I need allies. *Ireland* needs allies."

"I'm a humble farmer—"

"My friends believe you are Charlotte Dillon."

Charlotte chortles. "Your ghost pirate? And what do you believe?"

"I believe it, too."

At length, Charlotte shakes her head and stares into the middle distance. "Risings live on hope, no matter how fanciful. This is a fantasy."

"I'm correct, aren't I?"

Charlotte turns for the house, calling back, "You amuse me, monsieur. I thank you for the diversion."

"Madge Dixon."

That name sends a chill down Charlotte's spine, and she stops.

"Did she go down with your ship?" Heroux approaches. "Michael Dwyer would like to know."

Her voice shakes when she says, "I don't know any Madge Dixon. You have me confused with someone else."

"I think you do know her, and I'm even more certain now than I was a moment ago."

Charlotte is shaking with fear and anger when she turns back to Heroux with flinty eyes. "You don't know anything. Now I think it's time you leave."

The man nods reluctantly. "I won't give up."

Faire Abbey, Paris

While summer ripens in the hills of Montmartre, the heat of August presses in on Paris. On the second Monday of the month, James returns to the abbey, his heart beating out of his chest in excitement, keen to finally get the answers he seeks. But at the main gate, the abbess still shakes her head. "I've not yet heard from St. Croix, monsieur."

James's heart craters to his gut. "I don't..." He shakes his head, gathering his words. "I don't know how best to prove myself to you."

The abbess looks beyond James to Keogh.

"If I could have a word with you, Mother Abbess?" the big man asks.

The abbess nods and opens the door wide, letting Keogh through.

In the woman's office, they sit, and Keogh doesn't waste any time.

"Jamie is… imperfect. He hasn't always said the right thing to Charlotte. Lord knows he hasn't always done the right thing. But only because he has been in a desperate fight with himself.

"Have you ever wanted something in your heart that your place, that this world, wouldn't allow you to have?"

The abbess has, and her countenance softens.

"Jamie loves Charlotte and has from the first moment he laid eyes on her, but he couldn't have her, you see. His place and hers, his honor and hers, wouldn't allow it.

"Yes, they have fought, they've exchanged harsh words, and they've hurt each other. Both of them. But despite what you might believe of men, Jamie is no careless brute. He would never hurt her, not like that. And despite what you might believe of women, Charlotte is no helpless maiden. She gives as good as she gets.

"And Charlotte," he adds, "for all this mad flight, despite what she might've told you, she loves him, too. I know this without a shadow of a doubt."

"Why did she leave him, monsieur?"

"Jamie wanted to marry Charlotte, but his circumstance and hers made that impossible."

"And what makes their circumstances different now?"

"If Charlotte is calling herself Madam Beaumont…" Keogh notes a flicker of recognition on the abbess's face. "Then they not only share a love—they share a son. That changes everything." He pauses. "You know where they are, don't you?"

The abbess looks down at her desk.

"Don't you?" Keogh presses.

The woman stands and urges a reluctant Keogh to the door. "One month, monsieur."

"Please," he says, stopping at the door.

"Let me make another inquiry," the abbess says. "A woman nearby, and I promise when your Monsieur Blair returns in one month's time, even if I have not heard back from St. Croix, I shall have the answers he seeks, one way or another."

Keogh stops at the door. "Dillon."

"Monsieur?"

"We believe Charlotte Beaumont is actually Charlotte Dillon. If you should make this inquiry, please ask her about the name Dillon."

"Very well, monsieur."

When Keogh leaves, the abbess returns to her desk and begins to write.

Belle Mina, Montmartre

Days later, when Charlotte returns from a long, hot stroll through the vine rows with Jamie, Sidonie hands her a letter bearing the seal of the First Consul's wife.

Charlotte has received three separate letters from Madam Bonaparte since her note to the woman sent at the end of February. Warm, even enthusiastic, Josephine wrote about inanities at Malmaison and about her fruits and flowers, about her children and about her amusing friend Lieutenant Charles, always politely urging Charlotte and Jamie to come for a visit. This time, however, is different:

My Dearest Madam Beaumont,

I am recently in receipt of a most unexpected and intriguing letter. I'm afraid only you can set my curiosity at ease.

This coming Friday, my carriage shall arrive at noon in the Montmartre village square. I must insist you and Jamie come for a visit.

Your dearest friend,
Josephine

Cool, direct, and insistent, the note's tone leaves Charlotte no choice but to go. And not merely because Madam Bonaparte would brook no refusal, but also because of that mysterious letter. Monsieur Heroux must be plotting.

That Friday, Charlotte arrives in the village with Jamie to see a gleaming consul carriage waiting for her. The three-hour journey feels like an age. Charlotte wants to reach her destination and doesn't want to in equal measure. And at nearly ten months, Jamie won't be content to merely sit in his mother's arms. Crawling, climbing, and exploring, to him the large landau is an unforgiving cage.

When the carriage finally rolls to a stop at Malmaison, Charlotte and Jamie, red-faced and flustered, gratefully emerge.

"How good of you to come," Madam Bonaparte says in greeting, though her manner is more reserved than it has been. "Settle in. Refresh yourselves. I have arranged for a surprise at dinner."

Over the coming hours, Charlotte unpacks, sees to Jamie, and tries to nap, but her nerves are even more frayed. When she finally gives the baby over to a nursemaid and glides down for drinks, her heart is pounding loudly in her ears.

In the music room, Charlotte finds Madam Bonaparte dragging a careless hand along the white braids that crisscross Lieutenant Charles's coat front. Then he glimpses Charlotte and steps back, abashed. Josephine turns and, without a trace of shame, smiles brightly.

"Ah, my friend, Madam Beaumont." Josephine hands her a goblet of golden wine and leads her over to the lieutenant. "You must tell us all about Montmartre. Your château, your vines—leave nothing out."

This is more the Josephine Charlotte remembers from Christmas, and while she sips her wine and shares stories of her life, the edge of her nerves is blunted. The cocktail hour wanes, and Charlotte's mind is turning toward dinner when Madam Bonaparte looks at the door with a delighted smile.

"You've made it, monsieur."

There stands Monsieur Heroux in his regal green and gold. He nods to Madam Bonaparte, then looks to Charlotte, the expression on his face betraying nothing. Just then, a butler announces that dinner is served.

In the dining room, Madam Bonaparte sits at the head of the table, urging the lieutenant to sit on her right and Charlotte and Heroux to sit on her left. The dinner commences in amiable good cheer, the young lieutenant full of amusing stories that make Josephine laugh out loud. Finally, when the dessert is served, Madam Bonaparte pins Charlotte and Heroux with a searing gaze. "I think my good friends here have something to tell me?"

Charlotte and Heroux regard each other, then Heroux sits forward, clearing his throat, but Josephine says, "No," and flits her fingers. "Not you, monsieur. Not yet. I should like to hear what Madam *Beaumont*"—the woman adds the subtlest stress to the surname—"has to say on the letter."

"You've received a curious letter regarding me," Charlotte states.

Josephine nods.

"What did it say?"

Madam Bonaparte looks at Monsieur Heroux, then back to Charlotte. "Despite my husband's capable command, there are many who intrigue for a different France. Some who conspire to see a Bourbon restoration."

Lieutenant Charles scoffs, and Madam Bonaparte skewers him with her gaze. To this, he coughs and takes a drink until finally her quelling gaze makes him look keenly at his empty plate. Then she returns an indulgent look to Charlotte and Heroux.

"I like very much being amused." Josephine gives a side-eye to Charles. "And I'm always keen to be reminded of my childhood home. I have fond memories of Martinique, but I am not so amused as to be completely careless, or I should hope not. How do you know so much of the West Indies, madam?"

"I lived there."

Josephine nods. "You stayed at Faire, so you must have money. You're fluent in French, so you must have an education. Yet I think you are not a French captain's widow." Madam Bonaparte glances at Heroux. "Perhaps you know more of Monsieur Heroux's cause? Or shall I say 'Emmet'?"

The man's eyes flicker for only a moment, but Josephine merely smiles. "You have your spies, and I have mine, but you knew that, didn't you, Robert?" Then she turns back to Charlotte. "You, however, I thought an orphaned bird and didn't bother to set my spies on. Now here I am, caught out. I think perhaps your name is not Beaumont but Dillon."

Fear lances through Charlotte's heart, and her cheeks burns as she peers at Emmet.

"And perhaps," Josephine continues, "the father of that sweet boy upstairs is not dead but very much alive."

Charlotte shakes her head.

"Perhaps he is even looking for you."

Charlotte looks up at Josephine. "No."

"No?" The subtle smile that was on Madam Bonaparte's face widens. "To this point you are so certain."

When Charlotte says nothing, Josephine pronounces the dinner over. Then she whispers to Lieutenant Charles, who nods and suggests cigars and cognac to Monsieur Emmet.

"Now you must be very good boys," Madam Bonaparte says, smiling cheekily. When the men turn to leave, she adds, "Monsieur Emmet, worry not. While I cannot promise you his support, you shall still have my husband's ear."

In the orangerie, Madam Bonaparte is keen to show Charlotte her new roses, but Charlotte is only half there. Part of her remains in that dining room, in her chair when Josephine said her true name, when she proposed that James was searching for her. In truth, the mere suggestion made Charlotte flood with heat. No matter how long it's been, no matter how far she's gone, she still can't escape the stirrings that remain in her heart.

"Your name is Dillon, is it not?" Josephine asks, jarring Charlotte from her musings.

Charlotte blushes, and she's struck dumb with uncertainty. It's bad enough to perpetuate such a lie around any friend, but when that friend is the wife of the First Consul of France…

"Do you doubt my sympathies for a woman in a tenuous position?" Josephine asks.

Charlotte shakes her head and utters, "My name is Dillon."

"And if Jamie's father were alive, would you like to see him?"

Inexplicably, tears well in Charlotte's eyes. "But he isn't."

Madam Bonaparte puts a heavy hand on Charlotte's forearm and Charlotte looks at it. "Suppose he were, this man of which you spoke with such tenderness, this man you loved with all your heart. Suppose he were here, in France, this very night. Would you go to him? Would you run? Would you fly?"

With a peculiar mix of fear and exhilaration, Charlotte dreads what Robert might demand from her and wonders why Josephine seems so determined to suggest James might be here in France. After all this time, she assumed he let her go to find happiness with Jenny. Her throat is choked with emotion when she says, "Why do you ask me this, madam, when you know I grieve him?"

At length, Josephine scrutinizes Charlotte, then eventually she says, "Do you know why I have made a friend in Lieutenant Charles?"

Charlotte shakes her head.

"Like this rose, he is pretty. He amuses me so I am rarely lonely when the general is on his campaigns. Hippolyte craves a strong woman, an older woman, a woman who can take him in hand. He fancies himself strong, but behind closed doors, he is… something else." Madam Bonaparte beams in her musing. "Men like this are easy to collect. It is painless to pass time with someone who can never hurt you but not terribly satisfying, I think."

"I wouldn't know, madam."

"So, he did hurt you, then."

Again, Charlotte shakes her head.

"You haven't answered my question," Josephine says.

"What question?"

"If Jamie's father were here right now, would you run *from* him or *to* him?"

When tears crest and spill, Charlotte looks down and wipes them away. "I… I do miss him…"

Madam Bonaparte gently squeezes Charlotte's arm and gives her a tender smile.

Later, when Lieutenant Charles and Monsieur Emmet join the ladies in the orangerie, Charlotte pulls Emmet into a quiet corner. "You wrote to her about me?"

"Pardon me?" he asks.

"You needn't be coy anymore, Monsieur *Emmet*. I know you want my help. How else could she know my true background save from you?"

Robert glances at Josephine, who is smiling indulgently at her drunken young lieutenant. "Whatever she knows of you, madam, I swear to you on my honor, she didn't learn it from me."

14

That night, Charlotte lies awake, her heart pounding out of her chest as she hears Monsieur Emmet's words over and over again:

Whatever she knows of you, madam, I swear to you on my honor, she didn't learn it from me.

And Madam Bonaparte had been so insistent on the possibility that James might be in France. Charlotte has sensed that Josephine enjoys goading people, but this is more than goading—it's cruel...

Only if it's untrue, her heart whispers.

Charlotte could return to her rote excuses about fleeing for the baby's sake, for James to have a chance to be happy with Jenny, for her to have a chance to be happy without James. But for the first time, she can't seem to summon them. They feel empty compared to the weight of her longing.

Belle Mina, Montmartre

In early September, Charlotte stands with Lazare in the vine rows.

The old man plucks a grape and breaks it apart. "See how the seeds are browning? That means the grapes are ripening." He plucks some more and hands one to Charlotte. "We're looking for just the right combination of taste, sugar, and acidity."

The grape bursts warm and sweet in Charlotte's mouth, and she smiles in relief. Two weeks before, she returned from Malmaison keen to resume her simple life. Monsieur Emmet may try to enlist her in his cause, but being a mother to Jamie, growing and harvesting grapes, making juice and wine—these are the simple treasures she prizes now. Yet her feelings for James…

"Madam?" Lazare calls.

Holding a bag, Charlotte hurries to catch up. Today they are doing more than tasting—they are collecting samples to crush into juice.

Once they've picked several dozen grapes from many rows, Monsieur Gérard ham-fists the linen bag, crushing the juice into a cup for them to try. For Charlotte, the sweet juice holds little meaning, yet when Lazare smiles, she beams.

"Soon, madam," he declares. "Perhaps two weeks until your harvest begins. But now we must secure you a crew to do the work." At this, his face falls. "I'm afraid we're not getting the kind of responses we need."

"I'm offering the proper pay?" Charlotte asks.

"More than sufficient, madam, and that is moving some, but…"

"But?" she presses.

Lazare regards her with a sad look on his face. "Some people would rather grow grievance than grapes."

Charlotte returns to the farmhouse to find Dinah and Sidonie sitting with Jamie in the drawing room. At nearly ten and a half months, the baby is busy crawling over and through a mountain of pillows. Then he spies feet, and his little face ranges up. He smiles and points and drools. "Mama," he babbles, and Charlotte scoops him up, brushing his golden-blonde hair out of his eyes and kissing his cheeks.

"Does he need a haircut?" Charlotte asks, examining Jamie with a pang of sadness. The older he gets, the more she wants to keep him small.

"No," Sidonie says. "I love his locks."

"I do, too," Charlotte says.

"Well?" Dinah asks.

Charlotte slings Jamie onto her hip and grabs a carafe of golden grape juice. At this, Sidonie jumps up and collects cups, and together the women sample the juice.

"What do you think?" Charlotte asks, giving some to Jamie.

Sidonie smiles, and Dinah shrugs.

"What does Monsieur Gérard say?" Dinah asks.

"He's pleased. Two weeks, he said, until harvest. But we haven't a crew nearly large enough to complete the harvest within three weeks' time. Almost certainly some grapes will go bad," Charlotte adds. "All this work"—she sighs—"to lose some."

Madam Berger looks out a window and mutters a curse.

Village Square

Days later, Monsieur Gérard is nailing up work notices when he spies Madam Faucher trailing him and ripping them down.

"Madam," he says, striding over, "what are you about? Are you so lost in your bitterness that you have no regard for another's work?"

"'Tis you who are lost," she replies with a look of scorn on her face. "Everyone says it—that you're only half there."

Lazare looks around them. In the midst of a busy market day, villagers mill about, determined to look as if they aren't looking.

"Madam," he says with a regretful smile, "you wear your wound like a shroud. I pity you that you seem unable to let go because you've mistaken bitterness for justice. Meanwhile, I am old. I haven't the vigor to care enough what anyone thinks of me. But these people are tired," he says, indicating those who are no longer pretending to look away, "and hungry. They can't afford to scorn good coin to serve your spite. Let them live. Hm?"

Monsieur Gérard smiles pointedly at some villagers who are keenly watching. Then he snatches the notices from Madam Faucher and nails them back up.

Faire Abbey, Paris

On the second Monday in September, James sits in the abbess's office at precisely nine in the morning. In truth, he wanted to be there at seven, for he hardly slept the night before in anticipation. Once again his heart is pounding in his ears, and he can hear himself pleading, but he can only wait while the abbess sits and pulls out a letter.

"Monsieur Blair, I thank you for your patience. Please understand, it is my ministry to protect these women."

James's mouth is dry when he chokes out, "Yes, yes. Of course." He indicates the letter the woman holds.

"I made a special inquiry to a friend of the abbey. She was a former resident. Someone who knows intimately why a woman should seek such a refuge as this."

James nods.

"She happened to find a special affinity for a resident by the name of Charlotte Beaumont, a woman with deep-red hair and heavy with child who arrived to us from the West Indies in October."

James sits forward, his heart, if possible, beating faster still.

"This woman, she's informed me"—the abbess regards the letter she's fingering—"does, in fact, also go by the name Charlotte Dillon."

Emotion burns up James's throat and wells in his eyes.

"This woman has assured me that her friend, Charlotte Dillon, misses the father of her child, and I was inclined to give you this woman's name and address."

James's heart seizes. His mouth falls open, and he chokes out, "Was?"

"I was inclined to help you contact this woman who can give you Madam Dillon's place of residence, but then I finally received word from St. Croix…"

The abbess pulls another letter, worn from travel, from her drawer.

Horrified, James stares at the letter, then stammers, "Th-the governor-general is—"

"From your slave, Juneh." The abbess hands it to James:

Dear Mother Abbess,

I thank you for giving me the opportunity to give testimony on behalf of Master Blair. He surely the finest man I know. He kind to his labor like no man, and he love Charlotte with all his heart. I am certain, if he be allowed to find her, he tell her true.

And Charlotte, no matter how stubborn and foolish she is, she love him true. She not afraid of him. She afraid of loving him.

In humble service,
Juneh

Tears spill down James's cheeks, and embarrassed, he frantically wipes them away. Then he looks to the abbess.

"I said I was *inclined* to give you this woman's name and address until I received that letter," she says, indicating the one James holds. Then she smiles kindly. "But Juneh's words have made me certain, monsieur."

The abbess slides a name and address to James. "She awaits your response."

"M-madam Bonaparte?" he asks, reading it.

The abbess nods. "Do you know, she was raised on a sugar plantation?"

"N-no."

"She comes to the abbey, bearing her West Indian fruit that she cultivates in her orangerie here in France."

"General Bonaparte's wife has befriended my Charlotte," James says, astonished.

"Yes."

Belle Mina, Montmartre

Charlotte stands in the vine rows, the sun beating high and warm on her face. She traces the gnarled gray-brown cane up to the caramel-brown shoots bursting with waxy green leaves and dusky green grapes. There, she plucks one and puts it on her tongue, bites, and it bursts sweet and tart in her mouth.

When she goes to take another grape, hands, tawny from the sun, long and square and strong, are already there. Without thought and without care, her fingers lace through his as if being intertwined is their natural state.

Then her eyes skate up to meet his—James smiles tenderly, as if he has always been there.

Charlotte wakes and peers through the sandy early light to Jamie's crib. Only days from reaching eleven months old, he's been sleeping soundly through the night for months now, and he sleeps soundly now. Not Charlotte. Ever since returning from Malmaison, it's been like this, dreams of James coming more frequently, more vividly.

Shrugging off her exhaustion, Charlotte dresses and does up her hair to work. Today, harvest begins, and though she's resigned to working long days and nights to make up for the insufficient crew, though she's resigned herself to the fact that they'll certainly lose some grapes without the help she requires, still she's determined to show her son that his mama can work hard for him and for her dream.

In the kitchen, Charlotte feeds a sleepy Jamie while Sidonie builds a fire in the great hearth. Dinah gives Charlotte bread and cheese and juice, insisting she eat and drink. Smiling indulgently, Charlotte swallows a full glass of grape juice, and soon the bright sweetness sends a burst of energy surging through her veins.

"Cane juice," she says.

"Hm?" Dinah asks.

"The sugar in the cane juice made us work harder." She peers into her empty cup. "This feels the same."

When Charlotte heads for the fields, Dinah insists on accompanying her.

"Do you work, madam?" she asks.

"If I can wield shears, I can harvest grapes, and I mean to, if you'll allow."

"I'm happy to have you beside me, madam. These are your son's fields after all."

"No, my dear. They're yours now."

Then they crest a ridge and discover a dozen new faces in the vine rows.

"What is this?" Charlotte asks.

Monsieur Gérard, who stands beaming, says, "It seems the village would rather grow grapes."

Over the following days, more and more villagers come, sheepish but resolved. Many hands make grapes drop into buckets. Young and old pass down the rows, collecting the buckets and dumping them into great barrels. There, women hike up their skirts, wash their feet, and climb in to stomp.

One day into the second week, when the harvest is about at the halfway mark, Charlotte strolls past a barrel and sees Sidonie, red-cheeked and smiling while she stomps.

"Sidonie!" she calls with a wave. "Where is Jamie?"

"Just there, madam." She points to another girl near the barrel who is cooing and bouncing a delighted Jamie. "Join me!"

"Pardon me?" Charlotte asks.

"Have you stomped the grapes yet?" Sidonie asks.

"No."

"Blasphemy," Lazare calls out, approaching them. He indicates the great barrel. "Get in, Madam Beaumont."

Charlotte shakes her head.

"You have pruned and loved them. Now you crush them. The wine will be all the sweeter for it, I promise. Go on."

So, Charlotte hikes up her skirts, cleans her feet, and climbs in. At the tender, freezing-cold balls sliding up her legs, she gasps. "They're cold," she says, breathless.

"All the better to move you faster," Sidonie says. "Can you dance?"

"I can dance," Charlotte replies.

At that, they grab the barrel sides and kick up their heels, stomping and laughing while pulp oozes between their toes, grapes fall, and juice rises.

Then there's a commotion, and they stop and turn toward it. Red-faced, Béatrix Faucher strides down a vine row, muttering while she overturns buckets of newly cut grapes. Charlotte hurriedly climbs out of the barrel, following mere steps behind Monsieur Gérard as he stalks toward her.

"Madam!" Lazare calls. "What do you think you are doing? You've no right to disturb the peace of these vines."

Spying Gérard, Madam Faucher stops and glowers at him. "Peace?" she rages. "There can be no peace in these vines." The angry woman looks around at all the familiar faces. "What are you all doing here? The Bergers killed my François." Her gaze falls on Charlotte, and she seethes and spits, "What are you doing here?" Then she sees Dinah and hisses, "And you…"

"What are we doing here?" Madam Berger asks. "We're tired of being blinded by rage over something we cannot change. If I could, I would tell you to leave this place and take your hate with you, but Belle Mina belongs to Madam Beaumont now. It's not mine, and it certainly isn't yours."

Dinah and Béatrix glare at each other until Charlotte says, "I think you'd better leave."

Béatrix looks at all the villagers, pleading for support, but only finds blank stares. Then she sees Monsieur Gérard, who shakes his head. Finally, before her tears crest, she stalks away.

After the villagers return to their work, Charlotte looks at Dinah, then collects Jamie and, with Sidonie following close behind, returns to the château.

Much later, when the sun slips below the horizon and Sidonie has returned to the inn, there's a knock on the door. Charlotte slings Jamie onto her hip and answers it to see Madam Berger staring at her feet.

"Madam?" Charlotte asks. "I thought you'd gone home for the night."

"May I come in? Just for a moment?"

"Of course."

Charlotte steps back, and Dinah enters, remaining in the foyer. "I won't keep you. I just… I overstepped this afternoon with Madam Faucher. I'm sorry." She pauses, gathering her words. "My husband didn't mean to kill anyone. If you knew him, you'd know he was a gentle soul. But if you'd prefer I leave Belle Mina, I'll understand."

"I knew the story, Dinah. Monsieur Benoit told me the night I bought it. You didn't overstep. Still, I can't help but wonder why, after that, you would stay."

Dinah smiles dolefully. "We considered leaving. We wanted to. But to call in their debts when the wounds were still fresh…" She shakes her head. "Then my husband, René, died not even a year later. Whether from the shame of killing François Cadieux or of a broken heart, I couldn't say. His heart simply stopped.

"I was left to hold their debt alone. Without a husband or son to care for me, I needed their payments to live, and if I called them in, as I threatened, I would be dead now. Many days I wanted to die, but not enough, you see." She shrugs. "So, we are inextricably bound up in each other. They hated me, and I hated them, and we needed each other.

"Until you arrived, madam. When you helped me up, it was the first kind thing anyone in this village had done for me in a very long time." Tears well in Dinah's eyes.

"Oh, madam…" Charlotte feels a deep cut of sadness in her heart. "Why should I send you from this home? It was a most precious gift you gave me."

"So, you don't believe it cursed?"

"How could I? It's thriving, you see. These neglected vines only needed to be pruned and pointed toward the sun to remember."

15

Château de Malmaison

As soon as he left the abbess's office, James wrote immediately to Madam Bonaparte for an audience. The woman's reply came quickly, and her tone was eager, though her answer—that she would not be available until the first of October—was deeply disappointing. While he replied straight away, pleading merely for Charlotte's address, the woman's reply was equally swift and reassuring:

> *You shall see her and that darling boy of yours in due time, monsieur, but I'm afraid you must allow me to indulge my curiosity first.*

Finally, the day arrives, and as James's carriage pulls up to the wheat-colored château, he can scarcely contain his excitement or his nerves.

After he is settled, James is led to the orangerie, and there he stops, struck by the fragrance of Seven Stars. Strolling through the potted palms and flowers, he eventually finds Madam Bonaparte bent over a rose. At his footfalls, she straightens and regards him with a soft smile. With even features and chocolate-brown hair swept stylishly up, she is as beautiful as the rumors claim.

"Monsieur Blair," she says. "How good of you to come."

"I'm most glad for your invitation, madam."

Her smile widens. "I imagine you are. Come"—she indicates a tea table and chairs—"sit. You must tell me all about our West Indies."

James swallows a sigh and sits. At length, they drink and discuss her home and his, slaves and sugar and the rebellion on Saint-Domingue, the state of Europe and her husband's campaigns. Eventually, when there remains only an amber drop at the bottom of his cup, James smooths his napkin and pins the woman with a subtle look of pleading.

"But you would know of my friend, Madam Beaumont," Madam Bonaparte says.

"I would. Very much."

"She is your Charlotte Dillon, is she not?"

James nods. Just hearing Charlotte referred to as his makes his heart swell.

"It is plain to anyone who would care to see it that Charlotte misses you desperately, monsieur. What I can't help but wonder is why a woman who misses a man the way she misses you would so willingly leave him."

In the long days between Madam Bonaparte's invitation and now, James devoted himself to learning all he could of the woman so that if need be, he might sway her most effectively.

"I think you can love someone," he begins, "and know in your heart that you love her, yet resign yourself to the fact that you must marry someone else."

He regards her, and she nods.

"I think it must be very rare, indeed," James continues, "to love someone with your whole heart whom you may also marry."

"That kind of marriage is for the peasants, is it not?"

"Or for the brave."

"And you are now brave?" she asks.

"I hope so, madam."

Madam Bonaparte insists that James stay on through the Sabbath until eventually, on Monday, when the consul carriage is packed, he looks to her again with pleading eyes.

"She lives in the village of Montmartre. My driver knows the way."

And with the greatest anticipation he's ever known, James sets off. Now, when he's finally mere miles from Charlotte, the three-hour carriage ride that wheels through Paris and climbs north into the hills cut into vine rows seems like the longest of his life.

At the Montmartre village square, the driver stops. James leans out a window and inquires about Madam Beaumont's residence. While many villagers pause and gape at the carriage, a boy of ten indicates a road and tells the driver how to find her.

"Her farm is called Belle Mina," the boy adds, "but you won't be likely to find her at the house."

"Why not?" James asks.

"She's in the midst of harvest."

While the driver resumes his seat, James asks, "Harvest?"

The boy grows shrewd and turns cagey, so James dangles a coin for him to take. "What is she harvesting?"

Snatching the coin from James's fingers, the boy says, "Grapes, monsieur." Then he tips his hat and scamps off.

The carriage trundles out of the village square and moments later pulls to a stop before a buttercream-colored house covered in climbing vines that are turning an autumn red and shutters painted a soft cerulean blue.

On tremulous legs, James climbs out and ranges his gaze down the hill. There is a great number of people and much activity in the vine rows. Still, he looks toward the house, then goes to the front door.

Gathering his words, his heart thumping in his ears and his mouth gone dry, James swallows and knocks. He hears footfalls, then the door opens to reveal a round-cheeked girl balancing a blonde baby boy on her hip. At the striking image of himself rendered in a child, James loses his breath, and the baby squirrels into the girl for protection.

"May I help you, monsieur?" Sidonie asks.

The baby's fearful indigo eyes are riveted on James, measuring him, and James can scarcely look away.

"Y-yes," he utters. "Is Madam Beaumont here?"

Sidonie steps out onto the front doorstep and, with her chin, indicates the sloping fields. "Down there, monsieur. She's a small little madam with deep-red—"

"I know what she looks like. Thank you."

"If you give me your name, I could tell her you called on her. Or you could return this evening when she come back for the night."

"No, thank you, mademoiselle. I would find her now."

"As you please, monsieur."

James hesitates, unable to take his eyes off his son, resisting mightily the urge to reach out and touch him. Seeing this, Sidonie pulls back and cuddles the baby closer to her. James smiles warmly at them, then turns on a heel and heads for the vine rows. Exhilarated, his heart races.

My son!

So peculiar a thing to meet one's child and in such a way. James's legs are limp as they carry his great frame down the hill. Then he sees her. Charlotte's red hair, swept up in a kerchief, crests the top of a great barrel. She stands within, bobbing and laughing with another woman. Beside the barrel, juice runs from a spigot into a bucket. James knows next to nothing of harvesting grapes, but he does know what she's doing, and to him, it's quite possibly the most beautiful sight he's ever seen.

Prowling closer now, James stands right next to the barrel for some time, watching Charlotte jump and dance, watching the juice splat on her dress and face and hair while she is completely preoccupied with the joy of stomping.

Finally, James quells a laugh, clears his throat, and says, "Charlotte Dillon, must I always find you filthy?"

In the barrel, Charlotte freezes when she hears that voice. All her thoughts of James, all her dreams of him over the past year and a half, have not been so vivid as this. Her heart soars, and her blood races; her legs buckle even though she wants to run to him. Peering down into the golden grape soup at her calves, Charlotte steadies her nerves. Eventually, she lifts her eyes and meets James's gaze. He smiles tenderly, and she gulps at a lock of honey-blonde hair that's fallen boyishly on his forehead, at his deep-blue eyes skating all over her, at his great frame that once held her with such tenderness. Seeing him here on her hillside, emotion settles in her throat and arousal settles in her core. "What are you doing here?" she asks.

"I could ask you the same." They regard each other for a long, unhurried moment until he asks, "The boy... up at the house... is he...?"

Charlotte looks around them. People are gathering, including Monsieur Gérard and Madam Berger, who look questioningly, fearfully, up at her. There's no help for it. Charlotte climbs out of the barrel and hastily washes her legs, reassures Lazare and Dinah, and urges everyone back to work.

Striding past James, Charlotte brushes so close she catches a whiff of his singular fragrance, and the relief of it soothes her. Halfway to the house, once they've gained some privacy, James stops her. "You were never going to tell me about him, were you?"

The heart-wrenching pain in his voice makes guilt wash over her. Charlotte shakes her head, both because it is the terrible answer and because she can't believe it is.

"He is mine," James says.

Cheeks burning in shame, Charlotte meets his eyes. "He's ours."

James huffs and merely stares at Charlotte for a long moment. "What cruelty could I possibly have done to you that you would hide someone so dear to me? *Two.* The two dearest to me."

Tears well in Charlotte's eyes. "It isn't that simple."

"Is it not?"

"You don't think I wanted to tell you? I wanted desperately to tell you. In the hothouse when you came to my bedside, in your office negotiating the pass, on the veranda when you were smelling the tea leaves. So many times I wanted to tell you it clawed at my throat, I could hear myself saying the words…"

"So, why didn't you?"

"I know about Miss Cannon—"

"Caroline?"

"How she deceived you, pleading her belly."

"But in time you bore proof enough."

"In time? We had no time. Are you not married to Miss Lund?"

"No."

Charlotte can't contain a broken sob of relief. "Why?"

"Why? I could never marry anyone who wasn't you."

Tears spill down Charlotte's cheeks even as she shakes her head.

"Yes." James thumbs her tears away. "Have I really been so foolish? Have I said all the wrong things? Done all the wrong things? Held my heart so close you can't possibly see?

"I love *you*, Charlotte. I would use *any* excuse to marry you. A letter, a word, a blade of bloody grass. *Anything!*" He points at the house. "That boy—*our son*—is just the most precious reason I can conceive."

Again, Charlotte shakes her head, and James stills it, cupping her nape and claiming her lips in a kiss so desperate they're gasping and grasping. In that moment, at long last, there is no one but them.

When eventually they pull away to catch their breaths, James examines Charlotte, her bright cheeks and rosy lips, her wild, sticky hair and juice-stained dress.

"Marry me."

"What? You're mad." She turns to walk away, but he takes her arm.

"Almost certainly. Only marry me. Right here. Right now."

"I can't do that." Again, she turns to walk away.

"You would have our son remain a bastard?"

That stops Charlotte cold. "You wouldn't."

"I've done nothing, Madam *Beaumont*, but reveal your ruse for what it is."

The heat of frustration singes her cheeks, and more tears slip down.

"You wouldn't leave him so exposed," James adds.

"That's one of the very reasons I left. So he wouldn't be a bastard."

"If you had stayed, we could've been married long before you were delivered."

Now it's Charlotte's turn to huff, incredulous. "And Jenny's threat? Whatever became of that? What became of her? You speak as if this is all so simple now when it was so complicated then."

"A year and a half is a long time."

"Have you been searching for me all that time?"

"Will you walk with me?" he asks.

James extends his arm, and his simple request brings Charlotte back to that long-ago night in the village when he first asked to court her. But before she can respond, he adds, "Can we get him?"

Charlotte leads James to the house, and there they find Sidonie on the floor of the drawing room beside Jamie, who stands at a settee, clutching and side-stepping. The little boy looks up, smiles, and points, saying, "Mama."

Scooping him up, Charlotte plants a kiss on his cheek. Then she points at James. "Papa."

James is at a loss. The baby boy is curled into his mama, regarding him with round, fearful eyes. Still, James holds his hand out.

Charlotte places the baby's hand in James's large one and says, "Jamie, this is Jamie."

James tenderly grasps the doughy little hand.

Together they stroll down lanes, past vineyards and windmills and the abbey ruins. All the while, they recount their lives since she left, and all the while, the little boy regards his father with deep skepticism.

At the harrowing tale of the storm and James's amnesia, Charlotte is struck dumb. Finally, she says, "I'm so sorry you had to endure that. I can't even imagine it."

"After a while, enough things returned to me that I didn't feel so outside myself. Save you, that is. In truth, I didn't want to be reminded that I couldn't remember you."

They carry on, discussing Jenny, Lord Peter Fitzgibbon, even the Countess of Tyrconnell. And for long moments, Charlotte is rendered awestruck. "My mother had a sister? I can't credit it."

Finally, near the top of the butte, they stop. The brilliant blue sky has gone soft with the slipping sun, and their accounts have all been said.

James turns from the view of Paris to Charlotte holding a sleeping Jamie. He can't contain a smile, for this is the view he's imagined all these months. "So, you'll marry me now?"

"And return to Seven Stars?"

He was going to say, "Of course," but stops himself. "You have a life here."

Charlotte nods. "A beautiful vineyard and kind neighbors…"

"But you've missed me."

Heat floods into Charlotte's cheeks, and she looks down at her feet.

"Please don't deny it," James continues. "We've lost far too much time denying. You love me, and I love you." He pauses, waiting for her to say something, and when she doesn't, he says, "There are no longer any reasons for us to remain apart and every reason for us to be together."

"I gave up Belle Mina for you once. I don't want to do it again."

"So, tomorrow you'll show me your vineyard, and tomorrow night, or as soon as Keogh can get here, we'll—"

"Keogh is here? In France?"

James nods. "We'll be married."

"After all we've been through, can it really be that simple?"

"After all we've been through, it can *only* be that simple."

They return to an empty château, though Sidonie has left a *blanquette de veau* in the warm stove. Charlotte thrusts the baby, who is starting to wake, into James's unsteady arms and lights some lamps to brighten the kitchen. Unlacing the bodice of her dress, she wets a linen and scrubs her face and neck, her chest and underarms. "I should've done this before we left on our walk," she mutters. "The sticky grape juice seems to have collected every speck of dirt in our path."

Charlotte looks up to see James riveted by her, his mouth agape and his hold precarious as the baby squirms. Rolling her eyes, she closes his mouth, then repositions the baby, who peers frightfully up at him and whimpers.

Charlotte scoops some of the veal stew into a bowl and begins to mash while the baby's whimpers turn to crying.

"He doesn't like me," James says.

Charlotte glances at the pair. In truth, James bounces the baby on his knee, and his hold appears natural.

"Well, he's a very good judge of character," Charlotte taunts, and they exchange a smirk.

"Then I suspect you have him completely fooled by your…" James indicates Charlotte's still-gaping bodice, and she chortles.

"They can be singularly persuasive," she says, picking up the red-faced baby, strapping him into a tall chair built for a mite, and tucking a linen at his neck.

"They have been for me," James says.

They exchange another glance, this one thick with longing. Then Charlotte pulls the chair before James and says, "Would you like to feed him?"

"Please."

And with that, James begins to spoon-feed his son. Charlotte watches for some moments to see that his portions are small enough and his touch gentle, and all the while, the baby looks from each spoon of food to the man holding it, then to his mama. Seeing this, Charlotte places a tender hand on James's shoulder, and both the baby and his father pause to peer up at her.

"You see?" she says, pulling out a copper tub and lighting a fire under a kettle. "He's a very good judge of character." Then she grabs two large buckets and heads to the well.

When she returns a few moments later, James wears a delighted grin. "I was worried, when you walked out the door, that he would scream, but he likes his food."

"He is a mellow little fellow," Charlotte says, filling the tub and heading out for more.

When she returns, James says, "Wherever did he get that nature?"

"I couldn't say, since his father is so demanding."

"And his mother so incorrigible."

Charlotte goes to the well and back twice more, then pours the steaming water from the kettle into the tub and begins to shrug out of her dress.

James pauses in his feeding. "Do you bathe here, in the kitchen?"

"Can you think of a more suitable place to keep a tub and buckets?"

"I suppose not."

"Belle Mina is not such a grand place as Seven Stars. I haven't a housekeeper or cook. I have Sidonie and Dinah, and they are more than enough."

At her chemise, Charlotte pauses. She intended to be brazen in her nudity, but the memory that she's barely been nude with anyone—save for James and that was more than a year and a half ago—makes her suddenly reluctant.

"Shall I leave?"

"No...I..." Charlotte looks at James. She can feel her cheeks growing warm, and she curses herself, skims out of her chemise, and slips into the tub. "You'll have to excuse me," she says, soaping and scrubbing herself, "I wasn't planning on receiving any guests today, and I'm afraid I'm filthy."

The baby's bowl empty, James hands the wooden spoon to his son to chew, then sinks to the floor beside the tub. "I pray you never again apologize for stripping down to the buff before me."

Hastily clean, Charlotte sits back in the tub and wraps her arms around her knees. She glances at her son, who sits contentedly chewing and drooling, then looks at James with his arms folded over the rim of the tub.

"Do you remember?" she asks.

"That first night? How could I forget it?"

"You did forget it."

James looks at the water and utters, "I'm sorry."

Chagrined, Charlotte cradles his chin, urging him to look up. "No, *I'm* sorry. I shouldn't have said it. I pray you never again apologize for losing your memory. If it was anyone's fault, 'twas mine."

"'Twas that ill-mannered storm."

"Quite. We shall blame that storm."

Then James takes Charlotte's lips in a long, searing kiss. Heedless, soon James is taking off his cravat and unbuttoning his shirt.

"No," Charlotte breathes.

"No?" James asks.

Charlotte indicates the baby, who is quickly losing interest in the spoon. "I need to tend to him first."

Her shyness from earlier discarded, she grabs a linen and gets out, swiftly drying off with James's eyes fixed on her.

"I wish I had seen you heavy with child."

"'Twas nothing to see. I was a whale with red hair."

"Now *that* would have been something to see," he says. "I'll have to dedicate myself to placing you in that state again soon." Pulling her into his arms, he drags his lips from her ear down her neck.

The baby fusses, and Charlotte pulls away. "Jamie needs me."

"Yes, he does," James echoes, giving her a needful look.

"If we are to be together—"

"We are," he says.

"—then we must call one of you by a different name."

When Charlotte dons her clothes once more, James whines. "No. I had scarcely a glimpse. We're going in the wrong direction."

She puts a hand on his chest and gives him a cheeky smile. "Bide your time, sir. He'll be awake for a while." James looks pained, but Charlotte ignores him, starting a fire, serving their own meals, and placing some toys before the baby.

When they sit to eat, James says, "I feel helpless here. When may we leave?"

"What if I don't want to leave?"

James never considered this, and his pause is palpable until he says, "I must insist. I would have my wife and child with me."

"I'm not your wife yet."

"But you will be. When we returned from our walk, I sent the carriage to collect Keogh and inquired about a priest."

"And they shall be here…?"

"On the morrow. The day after at the latest."

"Then we have some decisions to make." Charlotte looks at James, who is resolute. "I'll not give this vineyard up, Jamie. It's in my name, and I would have it remain so."

"Tis a beautiful place. Truly. But I cannot live in France. I have a world of obligations at Seven Stars. And, in truth, I would miss it. I love cultivating sugar."

"I wanted to tell you… I've been wanting to tell you for some months… just how sorry I am."

"For which indiscretion now?" he says, winking.

"These vines, do you know that the arms are called canes?"

"No."

Charlotte nods. "Monsieur Gérard has been teaching me of grapes. When I felt these vines and these workers in my safekeeping, I knew, intimately, just how devastating my thieving was. You built far more than an enterprise of sugar for profit. I know that now, and I'm sorry."

James kisses Charlotte's hand and takes another bite of his veal stew.

"So, you must know," she continues, "how I'm coming to feel about Belle Mina."

"What shall we do then? I won't give you up."

They finish the meal and settle on the floor with the baby. After some time playing, James says, "How about Jay? It should be an easy enough change."

Charlotte regards the baby toddling with his little hands clutching James's fingers. "Yes. I like that." She peers wide-eyed into the baby's face. "Jay."

Sometime later, they retire upstairs, yet still Jay is squirrely.

"By now he's usually in bed for the night," Charlotte says while she changes his napkin. "He slept on the walk." She sighs. "We can try to get him to sleep, but..." She shrugs.

In truth, while James has been regarding her hungrily for some hours, Charlotte is glad for the distraction. Amidst the sloping walls of her bedroom, James stands at the center, where the roof is tallest. She regards him with a soft smile that he returns, all their wanting tucked away in those gazes. Then she settles into a rocking chair and puts Jay to her breast. Never did she imagine James here, and now everything, even the simple act of feeding her son, feels heightened by his presence.

For James, his heart relied on envisioning Charlotte and his baby for months now. Yet as real as this finally is, still his heart feels infinitely fuller than he ever could have imagined.

"I never saw you feeding him," he says, tentatively approaching.

"Pardon?"

"I imagined this dozens of times, but I don't know... I never saw you feeding him."

"I can cover up."

"No." He creeps closer. "It's… the most peculiar sensation, love and longing… I don't know what I'm saying, only I like it. I love it."

"I only feed him like this at night now. I think we both cherish it too much to give it up."

"I can leave you—"

"No," she says. "Unless you want to."

"No."

Eventually, the baby's blue eyes begin to droop until they close for the night. James hovers close, watching Charlotte rocking him until she says, "Would you like to hold him like this?"

"Yes."

With great care, they trade places. Settling in, James watches Jay's eyes bounce under their lids and his jaw move. "I have wanted you for a very long time," he says to Charlotte, though still riveted to his son. "So long and so much it's hard to credit the time when I didn't. I wanted this too, and yet," his throat is tight with emotion, "I never knew how much I wanted it until right this moment. Out of everything I've been given, this is the most precious gift of all. Thank you for my son."

Absently, James looks up and finds Charlotte standing before him in the bare. His mouth falls open, then he abruptly stands, suddenly keen to set the baby down. Charlotte points at the crib, and James gently unburdens himself, then he prowls to her, his gaze skating over her as he discards his own clothes.

"How could I ever have forgotten you?" he asks while his fingertips burn a trail around a breast and down her belly.

Then James takes Charlotte in his arms, and they devote themselves to remembering.

Early the next morning, Charlotte wakes in the still-dark bedroom with James's warmth at her back. Turning, she glimpses him and breathes in his singular scent, then peers up at the ceiling, thrilled and awed by it all. James's sudden arrival, introducing him to their son, everything he told her of Miss Lund and Lord Peter and her aunt—*an aunt!* Her mother had a sister, a woman who wants very much to know her. Of all the incredible things, she can hardly credit that. Yet most significant of all, he insists they marry and return to St. Croix.

Peeling James's arm from her waist, Charlotte steals from the bed, shrugs into a robe, and peeks through the shadowy light at the baby, who sleeps soundly. Then she walks to the window and looks out, watching while the orange dawn spreads over the blue-black hills below. She loves him. With all her heart, she does. If it were only that simple, she would have married him a long time ago, and he knows this well. But a woman can scarcely answer her heart and not be eclipsed by it. And this little vineyard—*her* vineyard—has already brought her great joy.

The bed creaks, and Charlotte straightens. Footsteps shuffle across the floor, then James wraps his arms around her waist and rests his head on her shoulder.

"I don't like falling asleep with my arms around you and waking to an empty bed. It feels like you've slipped through my fingers again."

"Would you be sad?" she asks.

"Do you doubt it?" he murmurs, brushing her nape with a kiss.

"No."

"Where shall we marry?" James asks, slipping her robe from her shoulders and pressing his body to hers while he drags his feverish hands up and down her torso. "Is there a church in the village?"

"What shall I do about this vineyard?"

His fingers skate around her nipple, then tug and tease.

"Perhaps we should marry there," he says, "right there in the vine rows."

Now his other hand trails down to her sex, and two fingers slip inside. She gasps. "You're distracting me."

"Yes," he says, dragging his own sex along hers. "Is there anything more important?" he taunts.

"Sometimes."

"But not right now. When you've lost your heart, when she slips from your grasp and your mind, you walk and breathe and live phantomlimbed. So, you'll have to forgive me if now I'm desperate to know and touch you, to feel you from the inside out."

James turns Charlotte around and rests her bottom against the sill, wraps her legs around his waist and presses inside her with a deep groan.

"Shh," she says, "you mustn't wake the baby."

James, his eyes heavy-lidded and his mouth agape, glances back into the room, then meets Charlotte's gaze with a triumphant smirk.

He makes love to her with long strokes and for long moments until they find their releases, then he kisses her neck, burrows his head there, and says, "How I've missed you."

"And I you." Charlotte wraps her arms around him, holding him tight, holding him tenderly while the morning dawns.

Eventually, she whispers, "I meant what I said, Jamie. I'll not sell Belle Mina."

Jay begins to babble, and James and Charlotte exchange a look of uncertainty, then turn to dress. A short time later, they go down and Charlotte introduces James to Dinah and Sidonie.

The pair regard him with kind confusion until he adds, "Her betrothed. You must join us for the wedding this evening." Now they look to Charlotte with plain confusion, and she smiles tightly.

After breakfast, Charlotte kisses the baby goodbye and drags James out of the house. The door is barely shut behind them when she says, "'Join us for the wedding this evening'? You're awfully certain of things."

"I'm certain I don't dare let you slip from my grasp again. I'm certain we love each other. I'm certain Jay needs a father, and I want desperately to be one. What is there to be uncertain about?"

Charlotte stops them before they reach the vine rows. "Where shall we live, Jamie? And before you say Seven Stars as if I'm an idiot, consider that just perhaps I'd like to stay here."

"Charlotte, please. We'll marry and soon—if for nothing else, for Jay. You know it must be done. You know it. Now do you honestly mean to marry me only for us to remain apart? Be reasonable."

"*I*? Why must *I* be reasonable?"

"It would be the first time. I know, but..."

He smirks, and her mouth falls open.

"Do you taunt me, sir?"

James tenderly cups Charlotte's florid face, and she stares steely-eyed up at him. "We're returning to Seven Stars," he whispers seductively.

"No." She slaps his hands away and stomps off for the vine rows.

"Charlotte!" James calls after her.

The laborers stop to gape as they stride past.

Monsieur Gérard attempts to stand in James's path. "Is something the matter, monsieur?"

But James skirts around him. "No. It's perfect." And in truth, to him, it is. He can't contain a growing smile as he stalks after her. His heart is so full it's threatening to burst right out of his chest; his blood is racing through his veins and pooling in his sex. He's never felt more alive.

"Charlotte Dillon, there is no one for me but you!" he calls out so that every person on the hilltop can hear. She stops and turns to him, wide-eyed and gape-mouthed in mortification. "I love you!" he shouts. "I have loved you with all my heart and soul from the moment we met. On that deck, when you were so filthy, when you put me in my place as if the sun would fall from the sky if you didn't, I knew I'd met my match.

"Think you I crossed an ocean for a milksop maid? No. So, fight me, only promise me you'll marry me."

Charlotte's face softens, and James strolls closer. "You love me, too," he continues. "Don't even try to deny it." He points at individual workers who are all looking on. "All your people here are watching."

Charlotte glances around them, and James nods.

"If you would keep Belle Mina, then you shall have it. If you want it in your name, you shall have it. The only thing I demand be in my name is you. You and Jay. You're mine. And if I have to declare it from here to Paris, I will."

Charlotte shakes her head, her cheeks burning and her eyes welling.

"If you would like to visit here, to come and stay for many months, we shall do it. I know nothing of being a vigneron, but you'll teach me."

Charlotte nods while tears slip down her cheeks now, and James wipes them away.

"And if, one day," he continues, "our second son—"
"Or daughter," she chides.
"*Or daughter* should like a vineyard in France…"
"She shall have it," Charlotte says.
"She shall have it," James agrees.

That evening, while the blaze-orange sun sets, casting the hillside vines in pinks and purples, James and Charlotte, with the baby curled around Charlotte's hip between them, stand before a priest on the edge of the vineyard. Under flickering torchlight and surrounded by Monsieurs Albert and Gérard, Madam Berger and the brothers Moreau, Sidonie and the rest of the Benoit family, the villagers who've come to harvest and Keogh who came up from Paris, they recite their vows to love and honor and to be each other's helpmates so long as they both shall live.

When the priest pronounces them man and wife, James and Charlotte turn to each other and, with the baby conspicuously between them, hesitate.

"For God's sake!" Keogh calls out. "Kiss her, Jamie!"

AUTHOR'S NOTE

When I first set out to draft *Ground Sweet as Sugar*, at the point of James's injury, the story diverged in my mind. I researched and made notes for his lost memory and a France arc but, in the end, decided the ending in *The Virtues of Vice* made greater sense for the overall story. That, therefore, is the official ending of the story.

Similarly, when I set out to write a bonus story for the collector's edition, I planned to write a prequel story, the love story of Charlotte's parents—Charlie Dillon and Anne Hamilton. Their story begins in Italy, and again, I researched and made notes, but in the end, the story wouldn't come. So, when I pulled back and asked my inspiration for the way, it handed me James, on that lighter, with no memory of Charlotte.

What a ride these two took me on! They always do. While I have notes for different arcs, I have no plans at this time to write any more in this world. I am truly grateful for the love you have for James and Charlotte.

The following are some additional notes on particular research for *Into the Complete Unknown*.

MEMORY LOSS Memory loss is as individual as a fingerprint. While I read a number of medical articles for my research, in the end, I borrowed heavily from personal accounts to create a realistic depiction of memory loss due to traumatic injury.

In particular, I was struck to learn the olfactory bulb has a direct connection to two brain areas strongly implicated in emotion and memory: the amygdala and the hippocampus. By contrast, visual, auditory, and tactile information do not pass through these brain areas. This is why a scent can so easily propel us back to a poignant person, place, or time, and it gave me an opportunity to once again use that fragrant handkerchief. Never could I have known when I first wrote that scene where James gives Charlotte that handkerchief just how important it would become.

FAIRE ABBEY While Faire is a fictional name, the depictions of the architecture, the residents, and its ministry are borrowed heavily from the very real Pentemont Abbey in Paris.

There were many famous residents of Pentemont, including Princess Louise Adélaïde de Bourbon and Thomas Jefferson's daughters, Martha and Mary, while he served as U.S. Minister to France. It also housed Josephine Bonaparte, known at the time as Rose de Beauharnais, and her two young children, Eugène and Hortense, during her tumultuous first marriage.

Pentemont, like many Cistercian abbeys, was dedicated to educating girls and protecting women and children from abusive arrangements. Sadly, it was disestablished during the French Revolution and turned over to the state. While much of it still stands today, it never returned to its original ministry.

MADAM LACHAPELLE In the labor and delivery scene in *The Virtues of Vice*, I found an opportunity to depict in fiction the very real-life change occurring in the practice of midwifery and obstetrics. Namely, that men and medicine were crowding into a space that had been almost wholly reserved for women and midwives.

A part of me felt sad about that because I love the characters of Abeni and Juneh and Luci and what they bring to Charlotte's understanding of her place in womanhood. Still, I felt an obligation to serve the history.

In researching Charlotte's options for delivery in Paris for *Into the Complete Unknown*, I was delighted to discover Marie-Louise Lachapelle. Performing complicated deliveries by the age of twelve, Lachapelle went on to become the head of obstetrics at the Hôtel-Dieu. She reorganized maternity wards, pioneering hygiene practices that reduced mother and child mortality rates. She developed a school for midwives that would earn them a degree from the École de Médicine, and she wrote and published textbooks on women's bodies, gynecology, and obstetrics.

Marie-Louise Lachapelle is generally regarded as the mother of modern obstetrics.

JOSEPHINE BONAPARTE Born and raised on a sugar plantation, taking refuge in an abbey, imprisoned for her relationship to a man considered dangerous to his country—I could not have written a fictional character more natural to become a friend to Charlotte Dillon than the real historical wife of Napoleon Bonaparte.

Napoleon's love for Josephine, demonstrated in his arduous and racy letters, is well known. Whether she returned that love is debated, for rumors abound about her various lovers. Her affinity for younger military men is well documented and, in particular, her affair with her hussar lieutenant, Hippolyte Charles.

While Napoleon divorced her to marry a woman who could bear him an heir, he made certain she retained her rank and title of empress, and it is rumored that one of his last words was "Josephine."

ROBERT EMMET Raised a member of the Protestant ruling class, Emmet's family nevertheless sympathized with Irish Republicans, including close family friend Theobald Wolfe Tone.

Inspired by Wolfe Tone's success gaining a French alliance for the Irish Rebellion of 1798, Emmet was in France under an assumed name during the time of this story, but I have fictionalized his time there. He returned to Ireland in the fall of 1802 without having secured an alliance.

The leader of the ill-fated Irish Rebellion of 1803, Emmet was captured before he could escape to France. Convicted and executed for treason, his "Speech from the Dock"—in particular, the final lines—secured him posthumous fame:

> *Let no man write my epitaph; for as no man who knows my motives dare now vindicate them, let not prejudice or ignorance asperse them. Let them and me rest in obscurity and peace, and my name remain uninscribed, until other times and other men can do justice to my character. When my country takes her place among the nations of the earth, then, and not till then, let my epitaph be written. I have done.*

THE BERGER MOBS In the revolutionary era, France confronted "the Jewish question" of rights and citizenship. For the first time, Jews were no longer required to pay special taxes and no longer confined to certain communities or professions. They would become full citizens of France, enjoying equal rights and protections.

Unfortunately, as a condition of finally granting these rights, the

French state required Jews to defer, some believed forgive, the repayment of debts Christian peasants owed to them. This confusion, combined with the sudden opportunity for ordinary French citizens to buy confiscated Catholic Church lands, spurred a rash of mobs—particularly in Alsace-Lorraine, where the vast majority of France's Jews lived at the time—in which Jewish families and properties were attacked.

So, while the Bergers and their specific story are fiction, they were inspired by actual events.

ACKNOWLEDGEMENTS

I am indebted to my invaluable friend and critique partner, Amber Hadley, and my dedicated editors, Kate Liebfried and Devon Burke.

Once again, I collaborated with the talented artists and designers at Qamber Designs & Media to bring this story to life.

My husband, Jeff, and sons, Teddy and Abe, keep me grounded and give me wings. They remind me what's really important.

ABOUT THE AUTHOR

Catherine C. Heywood is a bestselling author of romantic historical fiction and a former political speechwriter and communications consultant.

Raised in Red Wing, Minnesota, she studied international politics at the University of Edinburgh and has degrees in politics, writing, and communications from the University of St. Thomas and Boston College.

She explored the law and improv before settling on storytelling. Her worst job was scraping year-old tobacco spit off a shoe factory wall. Her best is doing this.

She lives in western Wisconsin with her husband and sons, and her interests include architecture and design, fashion and food.

Find out more:
www.catherinecheywood.com

Stay connected:
www.catherinecheywood.com/my-newsletter

CPSIA information can be obtained
at www.ICGtesting.com
Printed in the USA
BVHW081641160922
647222BV00010B/988